Ticking along with Swiss Kids

by Dianne Dicks and Katalin Fekete

illustrations by
Marc Locatelli

photographs by
Emanuel Ammon / AURA

Bergli
books

Published 2007 by
Bergli Books   Tel.: +41 61 373 27 77
Rümelinsplatz 19   Fax: +41 61 373 27 78
CH-4001 Basel   e-mail: info@bergli.ch
Switzerland   www.bergli.ch

ISBN 978-3-905252-15-6

In memory of

Angela Joos

1958 – 2005

the bookseller of Basel
who always enjoyed finding
just the right books for
children of all ages

THOMAS, ANGELA, SUSY

CHEEEEESE!

Thomas and Susy have just moved to Switzerland. They promised their Uncle George back home that they would write to him right away to tell him about their new life and what kids do here. They find it is such a confusing place with so many different languages and viewpoints. Their parents are new to it all too, and so busy with the move that they have little time to find out about the country and how things work.

Fortunately, Susy and Thomas meet Angela on their new playground. She becomes a friend like they've never had before. She loves reading books and enjoys finding interesting and fun things to tell Thomas and Susy about Switzerland.

Together they go through piles of Angela's books, explore the country, share experiences and discover all the essential things kids living in Switzerland need to know. Here's how it all began . . .

Table of contents

Table of contents

Are you new here?

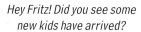

Hey Fritz! Did you see some
new kids have arrived?

Prehistoric people

Well, let's start at the beginning. Who discovered Switzerland?

Columbus, right? *The Vikings, right?* *No, the Romans!*

Stone Age
(150,000-4,000 BC)

In the 'Old' Stone Age (until 15,000 BC) people were living in caves above glaciers, as findings of skeletons show. They made tools of flint stones and hunted and gathered all kinds of berries and plants.

When the climate became milder, there were more forests. Then, during the 'Middle' Stone Age (15,000-8,000 BC), people started hunting small animals, caught fish and picked berries. They also made pottery and produced more sophisticated tools and weapons.

During the 'New' Stone Age (8,000-4,000 BC) people started farming and domesticating animals. They settled, built more permanent housing and crafted more specialized tools like ploughs.

Lakeside settlements
(4,000 BC-500 BC)

In the 4th millennium BC, people in what are now Neuchâtel, Biel, Zug, Zurich and Constance started building houses on stilts on the edge of lakes. The lakeside dwellers went hunting, fishing, grew grain and reared cows, sheep, goats, pigs and horses, which they used as working animals.

Pre-Romans and Romans

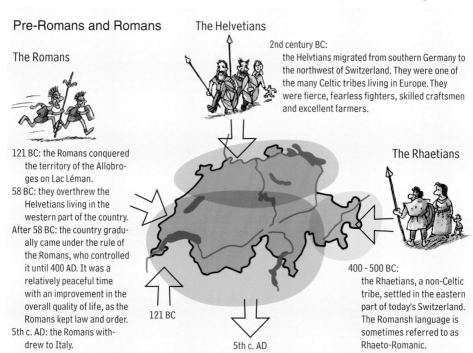

The Romans

121 BC: the Romans conquered the territory of the Allobroges on Lac Léman.
58 BC: they overthrew the Helvetians living in the western part of the country.
After 58 BC: the country gradually came under the rule of the Romans, who controlled it until 400 AD. It was a relatively peaceful time with an improvement in the overall quality of life, as the Romans kept law and order.
5th c. AD: the Romans withdrew to Italy.

The Helvetians

2nd century BC: the Helvtians migrated from southern Germany to the northwest of Switzerland. They were one of the many Celtic tribes living in Europe. They were fierce, fearless fighters, skilled craftsmen and excellent farmers.

The Rhaetians

400 - 500 BC: the Rhaetians, a non-Celtic tribe, settled in the eastern part of today's Switzerland. The Romansh language is sometimes referred to as Rhaeto-Romanic.

121 BC

5th c. AD

Prehistoric geography

Switzerland's landscape is very diverse. It's got high mountains, lots of rolling hills, plains and plateaus, U-shaped valleys and lots of lakes and rivers.

The Diavolezza area with Mount Palü

Hills around Menzingen, canton Zug

View from Weissenstein on the Aare

Juf in Averstal, canton Grisons

View from the Rigi over Lake Lucerne

But the landscape has not always looked like this.

About 600,000 years ago, the country was all covered in glaciers. Most of the territory of modern-day Switzerland, especially the Swiss plateau, was covered by a 500-1,200 meter-thick (1,640-3,937 feet) sheet of ice.

Morteratsch Glacier canton Grisons

In the course of time, the glaciers grew when it got colder and receded when it got warmer. During the interglacial periods, glaciers were melting and people started to settle down. But when the cold periods came, people packed up and left again.

These glacial and interglacial periods lasted several 10,000 years each. The last ice age ended about 10,000 years ago.

Glaciers left their marks on the landscape. Valleys were formed by erosion. Moraines came about when deposits of rocky debris were transported by the ice and piled up to form ridges.

When hiking around in the countryside and the Alps, keep your eyes open for pebbles, rocks and even huge boulders, so-called 'Findlinge', that look different from those around them. These different-looking rocks were carried along by glaciers miles from where they originated.

Huge 'Findling' in Flüelen

Go to the Glacier Garden in Lucerne to find out more about the Ice Age.

13

Landscape

Switzerland is a tiny landlocked country with high mountains, valleys, rolling hills, rivers, and lakes. Geographically, it can be divided into three regions.

In the area in green you find hills, a rolling mountain range and the watchmaking industry, which produces the world-famous Swatch watches.

The Jura hills
The midland plain
The alpine region

The part in beige is a hilly region with many lakes, rivers and excellent farmland. This is the area where most people live.

The most photographed mountain in Switzerland is the Matterhorn! (4,480 meters / 14,697 feet above sea level)

The blue part is where the high, steep mountains are, so there are fewer people living here.

Eiger, Mönch and Jungfrau are three of the highest mountains, but the highest Swiss peak is the Dufourspitze at 4,634 meters (15,203 feet) above sea level.

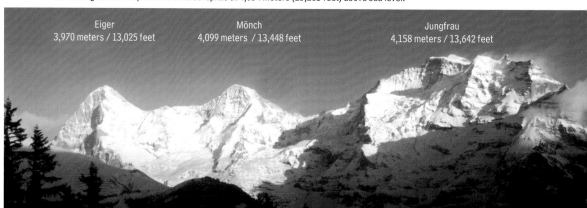

Eiger
3,970 meters / 13,025 feet

Mönch
4,099 meters / 13,448 feet

Jungfrau
4,158 meters / 13,642 feet

And what's that down there? It looks like snow.

That's the Aletsch Glacier, the longest and largest field of ice in the Alps.

The Aletsch Glacier is the longest (23.6 km / 14.7 miles) and largest in the Alps. It was declared a UNESCO World Heritage Site in 2001 and 2007. Other large glaciers are the Gorner Glacier (14.5 km / 9 miles) and the Rhone Glacier (9.1 km / 5.7 miles).

People built roads to reach the other side of important but dangerous mountains. First they traversed alpine passes by mules, later by horse-drawn carriages and nowadays by cars and bicycles.

Cool stuff! Pretty steep.

Sheep traffic-jam on a trail in the Aletsch region.

For real! The ones growing upwards are stalagmites and the ones hanging from the ceiling are stalagtites. Caves in Switzerland are full of them.

Are those pillars fake or for real?

You can find many caves in Switzerland. Hell Grottoes 'Höllgrotten' near Baar is a system of magnificent dripstone caves where you can wander through lit chambers and admire the fantastic limestone formations. 'Hölloch' in the Muotatal valley is at 193 km / 120 miles the longest cave system in Europe.

Rivers and lakes

Switzerland is a landlocked country, but there are many rivers and lakes.
Most rivers originate in the Alps. The Rhine is the longest river in Switzerland.

Lakes

1   Lac Léman (584 km²/226 square miles)
2   Lake Constance (539 km²/208 sq mi)
3   Lake Neuchâtel (218 km²/84 sq mi)
4   Lago Maggiore (212 km²/82 sq mi)
5   Lake Lucerne (114 km²/44 sq mi)
6   Lake Zurich (88 km²/34 sq mi)
7   Lake Lugano (48.8 km²/18.8 sq mi)
8   Lake Thun (48.4 km²/18.5 sq mi)
9   Lake Biel (40 km²/15 sq mi)
10 Lake Zug (38.2 km²/14.8 sq mi)
11 Lake Brienz (29.8 km²/11.5 sq mi)
12 Lake Walen (24.1 km²/9.3 sq mi)
13 Lake Murten (23 km²/8.9 sq mi)
14 Lake Sempach
     (14.5 km²/5.6 sq mi)

Rivers   *

15 Rhine (375 km/233 miles)
16 Aare (295 km/183 mi)
17 Rhône (264 km/164 mi)
18 Reuss (158 km/98 mi)
19 Linth-Limmat (140 km/87 mi)
20 Inn (104 km/65 mi)
21 Ticino (91 km/57 mi)
 *   distance to the border

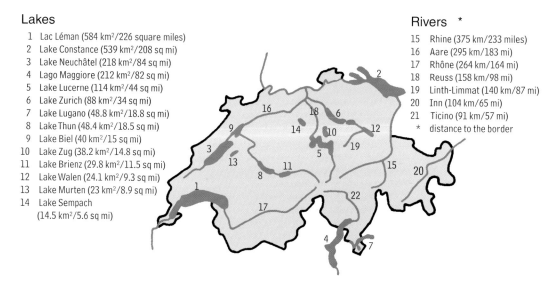

Water is the country's most important resource. It serves as drinking water, for the production of hydroelectric power and for leisure activities (swimming and refreshing boat trips).

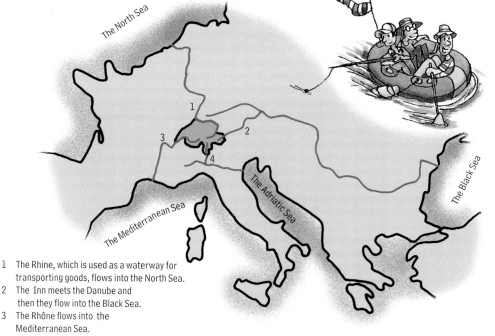

1   The Rhine, which is used as a waterway for
     transporting goods, flows into the North Sea.
2   The Inn meets the Danube and
     then they flow into the Black Sea.
3   The Rhône flows into the
     Mediterranean Sea.
4   The Ticino flows into the Adriatic Sea.

16

Paddle steamer on Lac Léman

Kids and adults of any age love to take boat trips on paddle steamers, be it on Lac Léman, Lake Lucerne or on any other of the many lakes in Switzerland.

View of the cityscape on the Lake of Lugano

View over Lake Lucerne from Mount Rigi

It's fun to hike in the mountains and to take pictures of the stunning views.

The Rhine Falls near Schaffhausen

Europe's largest falls are impressive. Visitors can watch the water cascade down from viewing platforms or from a boat at the bottom of the falls.

The castle of Chillon became famous when Lord Byron wrote 'The Prisoner of Chillon', a poem about Francois Bonivard who was imprisoned in the dungeon for four years. Have fun exploring the famous dungeon, the furnished rooms and the towers.

The Castle of Chillon, Montreux

Climate

When is it going to snow? I have never touched snow and my mom told me this white stuff is cold and fluffy. I can't wait to have a snowball fight!

Well, you have to wait a bit longer. Winter is still months away. I can show you in this book what it looks like.

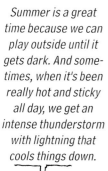

Summer is a great time because we can play outside until it gets dark. And sometimes, when it's been really hot and sticky all day, we get an intense thunderstorm with lightning that cools things down.

Spring
The days get longer and warmer. People feel invigorated by the sunshine after a long, cold winter and parks and playgrounds bustle with life once again. It may also rain quite a bit, sometimes even for days on end. Then a thick gray blanket of clouds covers the sky.

Summer
It's usually sunny and hot during the day and stays warm during the night. In summer you can often spot clouds like cotton wool balls or cauliflowers in the sky. When these clouds start towering, a thunderstorm is brewing. The best thing about summer is the long summer holiday. Schoolchildren get five to six weeks off, depending on the canton in which they live.

Waterspout
A 'Wasserhose' (waterspout) looks like a funnel of air, about 100-200 m (656 feet) in diameter, spinning around very fast. You don't see it very often in Switzerland, but there was one not long ago over Lake Constance.

Fruit trees blooming in canton Zug

Cumulus clouds are fair weather clouds that may produce light showers or rain.

Waterspout over Lake Constance (August 2006)

Fahrenheit   Celcius

Autumn
The days get shorter and cooler again and the leaves turn bright red, orange and yellow. Be also prepared for windy weather with heavy rains and storms. Sometimes the storms are severe like Lothar was in 1999, which caused mountain slides and falling trees.

'Hochnebel' (fog)
From November to February there is a thick layer of fog sitting like a lid on lower lying regions. Gray weather gets you down, but you only have to go up a mountain to be in the sun again.

Why is it so gray down here and where's the sun? I feel I have a cloud hanging over me.

Yes, that's what it is. You can't see the sun because of the fog. It's gray and cold down there, but sunny and bright up in the mountains.

Winter
The days are cold and short, snow falls, and some lakes freeze over completely, so children can go ice-skating.

Sea of fog, from the Üetliberg, Zurich

Records
TEMPERATURE: Highest: 41.5°C on 11 August 2003 in Grono (Grisons), where the average temperature usually hovers around 25°C. Lowest: -41.8°C on 12 January 1987 in La Brévine, the Swiss Siberia. The average temperature for January there is -3.8°C (1990-2006). It is the lowest temperature ever officially measured in Switzerland
RAIN: The largest amount of rain that fell in one day was 414 mm (16.3 inches) in Camedo (Ticino) on September 10, 1983. The average amount of rain on a very rainy day is between 30 and 70 mm (1.2 - 2.8 inches).
SNOW: In April 1999, the amount of snow measured on Säntis was 816 cm (27 feet). The average amount of snow from January till March that falls in the plateau is between 0 cm and 10 cm (0-3.9 inches).
HAILSTONES: The biggest hailstones found in Switzerland were 3-7 cm (1.2-2.8 inches) in diameter. They hit the Gantisch region and the Emmental in June 2006.

Clouds and their messages

The cirrus clouds are feathery, wispy clouds that predict fair weather.

Cirrostratus creates a ring around the sun or moon and brings rain or snow.

The 'Föhn' is a warm wind. When it blows, the view is extremely good and the mountains seem much closer than they actually are.
It mainly occurs north of the Alps and sooner or later brings bad weather.

A nimbostratus cloud looks like a thick black cloud covering the sky. It is a sign of bad weather, so if you see one of those ominous darkening clouds, get your raincoat.

Cumulonimbus clouds are giant heaps of clouds that produce showers and thunderstorms .

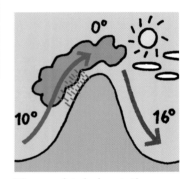

Warm, moist air rises to the mountain tops and loses its moisture. When the 'Föhn' blows down on the other side, it is warmer because of the compression of air.

The 'bise' is a cold north or northeast wind that usually blows for an uneven number of days (1, 3, 5 etc.). It can blow at any time of year, but is more common in winter.

In December, when the sky and all the clouds glow in a soft pink, angels are said to be baking biscuits.

Föhn – the mysterious warm wind

It makes some people giggle
Others get grumpy and blue
Some claim to be dizzy, some whizzy
You may not know what to do.

Some love its warm, sweet air
Its playful jumpy dives
Tickling your skin, packed with smells
And lovely delights for your eyes.

You can gaze at snowy peaks
Suddenly sharp and very clear
In a wink of your eye,
Surprise, surprise
The Föhn's brought them near.

The Föhn makes some people feel
Like skipping and jumping around
Into blue skies and sunshine
Never returning to ground.

It makes others scatterbrained
Moody and very confused
Have accidents, headaches and tantrums
And feel not at all amused.

The Föhn plays these silly tricks
But its warm winds are deceiving
It brings sooner or later for sure
Heavy rains when it's leaving.

This is what the Föhn can do.
What does it do to you?

Animals and flowers

Swiss kids don't have to go far to be around lots of animals. In many places you can stay overnight on farms or spend a vacation there and help care for the animals.

Swiss people love flowers of all kinds and you'll find endless varieties of them in the mountains, especially in spring and summer.

Bernese mountain dog

This is a funny looking animal, isn't it?

Donkey

Cow

Pig and piglet

Hen and rooster

Old MacDonald had a farm . . .

Sheep

Goats

Ibex

Marmots

Bearded vulture

Gentian

Crocus

Butterfly

Carline thistle

Edelweiss

Cyclamen

The ibex, marmot and bearded vulture live in the mountains. If you want to see them, you need to walk all the way up to the tree line or even a bit higher. Keep quiet, so you can hear the piercing whistles of the marmots.

Crocus, edelweiss, cyclamen and the carline thistle can also be found in the mountains. They look pretty, so one feels tempted to pick them. And that is exactly what many hikers did in the past. So there aren't too many of those plants left and that's why it's not allowed to pick them any longer.

Birds and fish

About 195 bird species regularly breed in Switzerland. You'll discover them in Swiss forests and alpine habitats, and a lot of them might be found right in your own neighborhood. When you are at lakes and rivers, keep your eyes open for fish too.

And their food is really lousy. There's nothing to beat mice.

Aren't my pecking sounds ten times better than their rap music?

Know what? Humans scare me to death.

Robin

Common buzzard

Great spotted woodpecker

Blue tit

We love eating the scraps off people's plates.

And borrowing their shiny stuff for my collection.

Yeah, but their constantly removing our graffiti is a real nuisance.

House sparrow

Blackbird

Magpie

White stork

Pigeon

Chaffinch

Slowworm

24

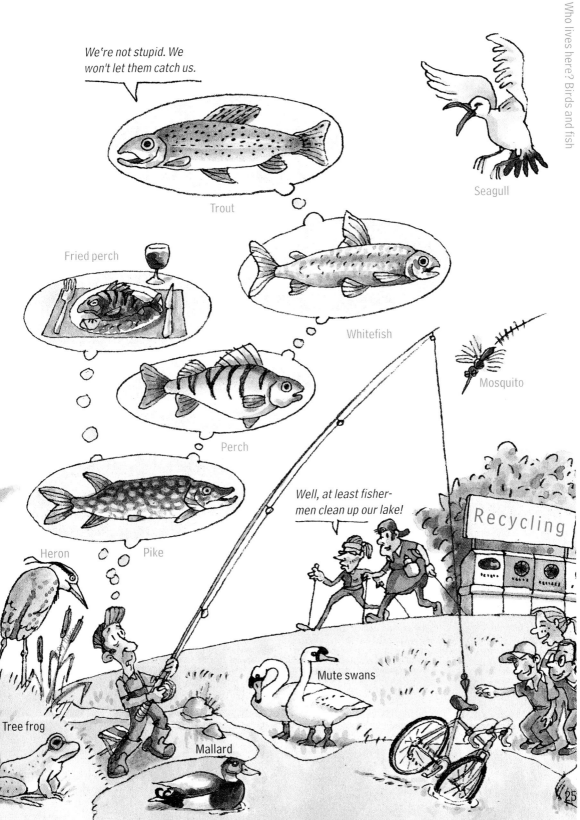

25

Forest and trees

Forests are an important part of Switzerland's vegetation, so you do not have to walk far to find a tree or a forest. About one third of the country is covered in forests. The south side of the Alps is particularly rich in vegetation. There is a rich variety of trees, at least 120 species. Norway spruce, beech and fir trees are the most common kinds of trees found in forests all over the country. And just like the people, many trees and colorful shrubs originated from other (even far-away) places.

North of the Alps

Swiss stone
pinecone

2,500 m
8,202 ft — A lot of Swiss stone pines and larches grow in the central Alps up to 2,500 m above sea level (cantons of Wallis and Grisons, for instance).

2,000 m
6,562 ft

1,900 m
6,234 ft — Spruce trees can be found in the Alps up to the treeline at an altitude of 1,900 m above sea level.

Beech leaf
and nut

1,500 m
4,921 ft

1,200 m
3,937 ft — Mixed forests, consisting of firs and beeches or maple and beeches, are very common around an altitude of 1,200 m above sea level, especially in the Jura hills and on the foothills of the Alps.

1,000 m
3,281 ft — Beech forests are widespread up to 1,200 m above sea level, especially in the Jura hills, the plateau and on the foothills of the Alps.

600 m
1,969 ft

Sycamore leaf

500 m
1,640 ft — Forests containing oaks and ironwood or beech can be found around the regions of Geneva and Basel.

400 m
1,312 ft

Oak leaves

Acorn

On the horizon to the north is Germany.

How far do we still have to go?

It's only 3,000 meters to the to

All the way to the south is Italy.

The climate south of the Alps in the canton of Ticino is milder and warmer than north of the Alps. This Mediterranean climate has an impact on the vegetation there.

Larch cone

South of the Alps

2,500 m
8,202 ft

Silver birch bark

Larch trees can be found in mountain valleys of the cantons of Valais and Ticino up to 2,100 m above sea level.

2,000 m
6,562 ft

Coniferous forests (spruce and fir trees), also mixed with beeches, oaks and pine trees, grow up to 1,900 m above sea level.

1,900 m
6,234 ft

Silver birch leaves

1,500 m
4,921 ft

Silver birch fruits

Deciduous forests (birches, elms, beeches) are common in valleys up to 1,200 m above sea level. There you can also find chestnut, hazelnut and walnut trees — kids love to collect and eat the nuts in autumn.

1,200 m
3,937 ft

Sweet chestnut tree

1,000 m
3,281 ft

Beech forests thrive at an altitude of 900 m up to 1,400 m above sea level.

900 m
2,953 ft

Conkers

Palm trees as well as lemon and orange trees thrive in the canton of Ticino. As for flowers, you can find camellias, azaleas and mimosas in gardens and in front of houses.

500 m
1,640 ft

400 m
1,312 ft

27

People and culture

You don't have to travel far within Switzerland to feel like you are suddenly in a different country. And it is not only the language that differs! There are different attitudes to life and getting along. For example, in the German-speaking part of Switzerland people are said to be very orderly and pay great attention to details like punctuality. In the French- and Italian-speaking parts of the country people are said to be more relaxed about being on time and easy-going about always having things in perfect order. Swiss people themselves enjoy talking about these differences.

Hello, dear. Daddy and I have been waiting for you. Wash your hands and come to the table.

Lunch in the German-speaking part

Salut Cheri! How was school today? Did you have a good time? I'm fixing something special today and lunch will be ready in a few minutes.

Can I stir the sauce?

Lunch in the French-speaking part

Gazola! Grandpapa is eating with us today and hopes to have time for a game of chess with you before you return to school.

Ciao, what's for lunch?

Salve Franco!

Lunch in the Italian-speaking part

People and language

Wherever you go in Switzerland you'll find other kids from all over the world. When they ask you what your name is, it is like a game of sounds. If someone asks you something like this, you only have to say your name!

What's your name?

Russian — Kak tebya zawut?

I sminiz ne? — Turkish

Jak masz na imie? — Polish

Hoe heet jij? — Dutch

Jak se jmenuješ? — Czech

Comment tu t'appelles ? — French

Ma ismika? — Arabic

Nin guixing? — Chinese

Wiä haissisch? — Swiss German

Come ti chiami?

Co has Ti num? — Romansh

Italian

Portuguese — Como se chama?

Albanian — Si te quajne?

Wie heisst Du? — German

Ma shimkha? — Hebrew

¿Como te llamas? — Spanish

Kako se zovete? — Serbian

Namae wa nan desu ka? — Japanese

Mikä sinun nimesi on? — Finnish

ungGa pEru enna? — Tamil

Vad heter du? — Swedish

Röstigraben

'Rösti' or 'Roesti' is a dish of fried potatoes. It makes a hearty meal and it is loved all over the country, but especially in the German-speaking part, where it originated. In the French-speaking part, it is said that people prefer to eat raclette. There is an invisible boundary cutting through the country that separates the Rösti eaters from the Raclette eaters and this dividing line is referred to as a barrier 'Röstigraben' or 'Rideau de rösti'. This symbolic 'Röstigraben' refers to the cultural and sometimes political differences between the Swiss German and French- and Italian-speaking people of Switzerland. The two groups enjoy poking fun at each other.

Nobody knows why Globi (a popular Swiss cartoon character loved for generations by German-speaking Swiss) is hardly known in the French-speaking part. Also in the German-speaking part there has been a very successful Swiss TV series and cartoon figure named Pingu which has had no equivalent in the French-speaking part of the country.

You also find that some traditional games like 'Schwingen' (Swiss wrestling), rope-pulling, 'Steinheben' (lifting stones) and 'Steinstossen' (pitching very heavy stones) are a lot more popular in the German-speaking part than in the French-speaking part of Switzerland.

The 'Röstigraben' is not a real border on the map and (so far) not a tourist site.

Fondue and raclette used to be found only in the French-speaking part of Switzerland but now it is popular all over the country and has been adapted by many cooks around the world.

How to make Rösti for approximately four people:

Ingredients:
750 g new potatoes (about 8-10 medium-sized potatoes used for making potato salad) salt, 50 g butter, 2 tsp oil

Preparation:

Scrub and rinse the potatoes. Put them in a saucepan, cover with water and add 1 teaspoon salt. Bring the water to a boil and cook the potatoes until tender. Pour off the excess water and let the potatoes cool. Remove the skins with a small knife, take a Rösti or cheese grater that has large holes to grate the potatoes into fine shavings. Add salt and pepper. Heat HALF of the butter and oil in a big non-stick frying pan until the butter foams. Tip the potatoes into the pan and press them with a spatula to make a nice neat cake. Fry for about 10 minutes until a good golden crust forms underneath. Take the pan off the heat and place a large plate upside down on top of the pan (you may want someone to help you with this). Tip the Rösti onto the plate with the golden side up. Heat the rest of the butter and oil in the pan and slide the Rösti back into the pan, golden side uppermost. Fry it for another 10 minutes until the underside gets nice and brown too.

Clothing and objects you need

Hiking boots – otherwise your feet might hurt on rocky paths.

You need a gym bag to take with you to school on those days you have sports – otherwise you'll look funny when everyone else looks sporty.

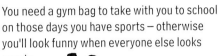

Rain coat, rain hat, rain boots – otherwise you might get wet and cold.

In kindergarten you need a 'Chindsgisack' – otherwise you might lose your apple for snack-time.

Swimming suit or trunks – otherwise you can't join others on the picnic who are swimming.

When you go biking you need a helmet – otherwise you might have to wear a horrible bandage on your head.

Since the weather changes quickly, it is good to dress in the 'onion-style' with lots of layers (warm jacket, under which you have a long-sleeved sweater, under which you have a T-shirt) so that you are neither too hot nor too cold.

Get ice skates, skis and a sled – otherwise you won't enjoy winter and snow.

And don't forget your skateboard, scooter, favorite game or toy.

Who is the most important Swiss?

Who's that guy standing next to the pedestal?

And what are they discussing?

That's Pestalozzi. He ... Shush, they are talking about important people in Switzerland. Let's listen.

It must be Henri Dunant, the founder of the Red Cross.

Hey listen. What about Zwingli and Calvin, the two influential reformers in Zurich and Geneva?

You're all wrong! Daniel Peter is the winner. He invented milk chocolate, the most famous Swiss product! And Henri Nestlé, of course, the inventor of powdered milk.

Hands up, who doesn't have a Swiss army knife? See, so it's Karl Elsener, who founded Victorinox.

And what would you do without your Logitech mouse? Daniel Borel is the winner!

Not worth mentioning! But Bircher-Benner's Birchermüesli is on every menu, even abroad.

I bet it's the Caran d'Ache guy Arnold Schweitzer.

No no no, I'm pretty sure the car industry would have gone nowhere without Chevrolet!

He doesn't count, he went to the US. I bet it's George Mestral, who invented Velcro straps for shoes.

How about you Mr. Pestalozzi? You started the program to provide education for all children!

It's Roger Federer, the great Swiss tennis player.

Bircher-Benner, Maximilian Oskar (1867-1939): physician who invented Bircher-müesli.

Borel, Daniel (1950): founder of Logitech and the mouse.

Calvin, Jean (1509-1564): reformer in Geneva.

Chevrolet, Louis-Joseph (1878-1941): motor racer, car maker, and designer of the first Chevrolet car.

Dunant, Henri (1828-1910): Swiss philanthropist born in Geneva, founder of the Red Cross.

Dürrenmatt, Friedrich (1921-1990): dramatist and novelist who wrote the famous play 'The Visit' (1956).

Elsener, Karl (1860-1918): cutler and founder of the knife factory that became Victorinox.

Euler, Leonhard (1707-1783): famous Swiss mathematician and physicist.

Federer, Roger (1981): one of the all-time greatest male tennis players in the world.

Giacometti, Alberto (1901-1966): sculptor, painter, graphic artist and poet.

Hayek, Nicolas (1928): entrepreneur and founder of Swatch Watch.

Klee, Paul (1879-1940): painter, watercolorist and etcher. He created modern, rather abstract works with fantastic and childlike symbols.

Kudelski, Stefan (1929): founder of Kudelski, one of the world's leading companies in digital security.

Mestral, George de (1907-1990): inventor of the widely used Velcro straps for shoes, etc.

Nestlé, Henri (1814-1890): industrialist and founder of the food and beverage company Nestlé.

Paracelsus, Philippus Aureolus (1493?-1541): physician who claimed that diseases were caused by external factors and not by an imbalance of bodily fluids. He was the first physician to use and prescribe drugs.

Pestalozzi, Johann Heinrich (1746-1827): Swiss educational reformer, he pioneered education for poor children.

Peter, Daniel (1836-1919): chocolate maker and entrepreneur.

Piccard, Bertrand (1958): scientist and hot-air balloonist. His father, Jacques, and grandfather, Auguste, were scientists and adventurers too.

Schweitzer, Arnold (1885-1947): entrepreneur, founder of Caran d'Ache and manufacturer of pencils.

Zwingli, Huldrych (1484-1531): reformer in Zurich.

Who is the most important Swiss? Who should be on the pedestal? What have you decided?

Wow! I didn't know there were so many famous Swiss.

Sure, there are. Some are born Swiss, but many have a parent or ancestor who came from someplace else. There are also many famous people from abroad coming to live in or visit Switzerland.

How do people understand each other?

English	German	Swiss German
Hello	Hallo	Hoi
Goodbye	Tschüss	Tschüss
What's your name?	Wie heisst du?	Wiä häissisch?
Where do you live?	Wo wohnst du?	Wo wonsch?
What are you doing?	Was machst du?	Was machsch?
Help!	Hilfe!	Hilfe!
Please	Bitte	Bitte
Yes/no	Ja/Nein	Ja/Näi
Thank you	Danke	Danke
Stop it!	Hör auf!	Hör uuf!
Will you play with me?	Willst du mit mir spielen?	Wetsch mit mir spile?
May I have that shovel?	Darf ich diese Schaufel haben?	Chan i die Schufle ha?
It's my turn	Ich bin dran	Ich bi dra
Bless you!	Gesundheit!	Gsundhait!

Chuchichäschtli (pronounced something like koo-ki-kescht-ly) means kitchen cupboard and only real Swiss kids can say it properly.

There are four national languages (German, French, Italian and Romansh) in Switzerland. English is also widely spoken and children learn at least one other national language at school. But there are also oodles of dialects that aren't always easy to understand. Have a look at the words in the table to find out what they mean in the other languages.

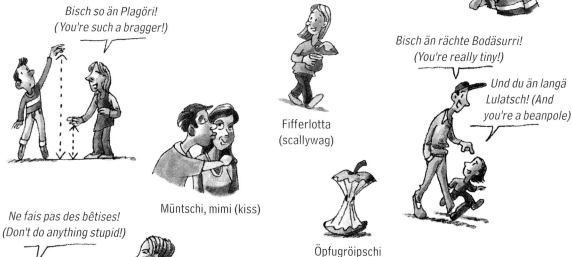

Bisch so än Plagöri!
(You're such a bragger!)

Bisch än rächte Bodäsurri!
(You're really tiny!)

Und du än langä
Lulatsch! (And
you're a beanpole)

Fifferlotta
(scallywag)

Müntschi, mimi (kiss)

Öpfugröipschi
(apple core)

Dai! (Come on!)

Ne fais pas des bêtises!
(Don't do anything stupid!)

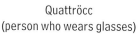

Quattröcc
(person who wears glasses)

French	Italian	Romansh
Salut	Ciao	Chau
Au revoir	Arrivederci	A revair
Comment tu t'appelles?	Come ti chiami?	Co has ti num?
Ou est-ce que tu habites?	Dove abiti?	Nua stattas ti?
Qu'est-ce que tu fais?	Cosa stai facendo?	Tge fas ti?
À l'aide!	Aiuto!	Agid!
S'il te plaît	Please	Per plaschair
Oui/non	Si/no	Gea/na
Merci	Grazie	Grazia
Arrête!	Basta!	Smetta cun quai!
Tu joues avec moi?	Vuoi giocare con me?	Vuls giugar cun mai?
Je peux avoir cette pelle?	Posso avere quella pala?	Poss jau avair questa pala?
C'est mon tour	Tocca a me	Jau vegn vidlonder
Santé!	Salute!	Viva!

In general Swiss people are very polite and they expect you to be too. So be well-behaved, watch your language, mind your words and watch your tone. Talking to adults is an entirely different story. If you are a child and want to address an older person you don't know well, then you are expected to use the polite form 'Sie'/'Vous'/'Lei'/'Vus'.

Horca la tatta! (For goodness' sake!)

... joggen ... Sneakers, Sweater ...

.... trendy ....

... Inline-Skates

... label .... cool ....

... Computer gecrasht ...

.... jeans

gamen ... surfen

Hey cool, Swiss German is just like English! Real easy.

What do grown-ups do here?

You'll find all kinds of different jobs to be done in Switzerland. Can you tell what all the figures in the picture are doing while they run around the country?

What jobs do people in your family do? Can you find them in the picture?

accountant
architect
baker
banker
bookseller
butcher
carpenter
cheesemaker
chemist
cook
diplomat
dentist
designer
doctor
engineer
farmer
forester
gardener
geologist
information technology specialist
insurance professional
journalist
lawyer
management consultant
meteorologist
musician
nurse
pharmacist
pastry maker
scientist
shop assistant
ski instructor
teacher
tourism manager
veterinary
watch maker, and many many more …

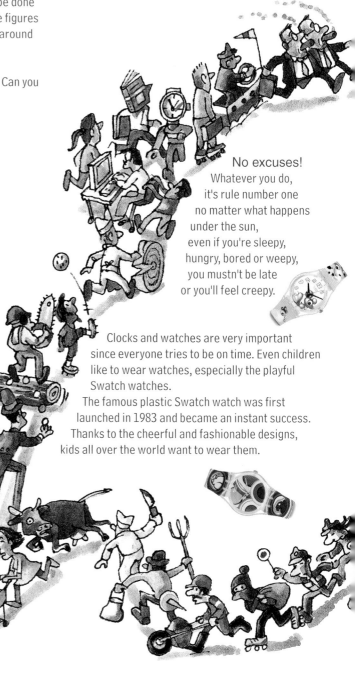

No excuses!
Whatever you do,
it's rule number one
no matter what happens
under the sun,
even if you're sleepy,
hungry, bored or weepy,
you mustn't be late
or you'll feel creepy.

Clocks and watches are very important since everyone tries to be on time. Even children like to wear watches, especially the playful Swatch watches.
The famous plastic Swatch watch was first launched in 1983 and became an instant success. Thanks to the cheerful and fashionable designs, kids all over the world want to wear them.

I MUSTN'T BE LATE!

Does anyone have time for anything other than work?

Nope, don't think so.

Watch out!
On timetables:
1 o'clock pm = 13.00
2 o'clock pm = 14.00, etc.
3.30 pm = 15.30, etc.
up to midnight = 24.00!

Some misunderstandings

Capital?

Geneva is not the capital of Switzerland, nor is Zurich — it's Berne.

Cuckoo clocks?

"In Italy for thirty years under the Borgias they had warfare, terror, murder, bloodshed – but they produced Michelangelo, Leonardo da Vinci, and the Renaissance. In Switzerland they had brotherly love, 500 years of democracy and peace, and what did that produce? The cuckoo clock. So long, Holly." -— The Third Man

This quote by Graham Greene was put in the film by Orson Welles who copied it from the Italian dictator Benito Mussolini. Whatever, the statement is not true! Cuckoo clocks come from the Black Forest in Germany and are usually not found in Swiss homes.

Yodeling?

Not all Swiss yodel! Yodeling used to be a way of communicating from mountain peak to mountain peak, then became part of Swiss folk music.

What is yodeling? It is a way of singing, especially when you change your voice quickly from your chest to falsetto. Herdsmen would yodel to round up their sheep or cattle. A 'Naturjodel' is when one or more voices sing a melody without words or meaning. But there are many songs to yodel that have lyrics and refrains. One of the most popular is the Rigi song:

> Vo Luzern uf Weggis zue, ...
> Te-o-la-de-i, Te-o la-de-o
> Brucht me weder Strümpf no Schueh.
> Te-o-la-de-i, Te-o la-de-o
>
> From Lucerne to Weggis there
> Yo-del-ye-hi-ho, yo-del-ye-hi-ho
> Shoes and stockings we'll not wear
> Yo-del-ye-hi-ho, yo-del-ye-hi-ho

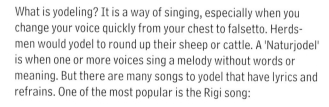

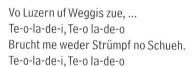

It's fun to yodel when you are in a rocky gorge or someplace where there is a cliff or rocks in the distance so that there is an echo.

Swiss steak?

Americans are surprised to find that there is no such thing as a Swiss steak in Switzerland. Nowhere in the country is there a common recipe to take a piece of round (tougher) steak, brown it in a pan, then braise it in tomato sauce. The name comes from a process of swissing meat, which means you pound it with a tenderizing hammer or put it through a device with rollers that have little blades. Another thing that can cause confusion: a lot of Swiss people pronounce 'steak' like it rhymes with 'peak'.

Swiss roll?

The English are surprised to meet blank faces when they ask for a Swiss roll in pastry shops around the country. They expect to find a sponge cake that has been baked in a shallow pan, then rolled up to give it a filling of whipped cream or jam, then cut into slices. This cake exists in Switzerland but it is called by different names like 'Schwarzwälder Roulade' or something similar, but is not considered to be particularly 'Swiss'.

Peaceful Swiss?

The Swiss were always good at fighting. Many of their communities had warriors trained and equipped to fight and these groups were sometimes hired out to places in Europe as mercenaries (professional soldiers). They were very fierce and used pikes (long spears of 3 to 4 meters) and halberds (two-handed poles that had an axe with a hook that enabled them to poke or pull enemy knights off their horses).

It is a myth that Switzerland has had hundreds of years of peace. That would be nice. But if you go to school in Switzerland, you will learn about the Battle of Morgarten (1315), the Battle of Sempach (1386), the Battle of St. Jacob (1444) and a number of quarrels caused by the Reformation of the Roman Catholic church. And some battles of Napoleon against Austria and Russia were fought in Switzerland (1798-1802) too.

Weapons?

It is true that today most able-bodied Swiss male citizens serve in the Swiss army, civil defense or community service. Military service is voluntary for women. And it is true that Swiss soldiers keep their rifles at home and you might see them on buses and trams going to shooting practice. Even though there may be so many guns around, Switzerland is still considered one of the most peaceful countries in the world.

Tourism

Why do so many tourists want to come to Switzerland?

That's a hard question. Whew! I'll have to think about that.

Did you find out?

Sort of.

What does that mean?

Well, first no one wanted to come to Switzerland because the mountains were scary. People thought life was dangerous and wild here. Then, some romantics started writing poetry about the beautiful views and the simple life of the people in the Alps. Suddenly it became fashionable for kings and queens and important people from all over Europe and beyond to come here to see the paradise of the Alps. At first, they travelled by horse-drawn coaches, or were carried up the mountains in sedans.

You mean they had cars back then?

No, a sedan chair is what you call the contraption people sat in while being carried up steep paths by porters. For a fee of course.

That sounds like fun!

Sure, if you are the one being carried. But even so, the peasants found it easier and more profitable to lug these tourists up mountains to get alpine views than to get their sheep and goats to where they'd find enough grass.

Sedan

Hotels were built on mountain tops and remote places, then roads and railways were constructed to get people to them. Eventually a lot of British people who loved sports came here to climb even the toughest mountains and have ski races.

This train goes up to Stoos in canton Schwyz, partially on cogwheels where the mountain is very steep.

So it was like a big Disneyland? Lots of fun?

Is that why there are so many unusual sports here like canyon jumping, kite surfing, glacier bungy, ice climbing, airboarding, and zorbing. I googled these sports and discovered that the wildest of things are done here!

Yes, and no. It was risky to build all those railways and tunnels and hard to get everyone to agree about where they would be, how they could be made safe, and who would pay for it all.

An old newspaper article from 1887 about emigrants to the U.S.

There were times in Switzerland when there wasn't enough food and life was so hard that many Swiss left to find a better life in other countries. You had to be clever and have good ideas to survive.

Shopping

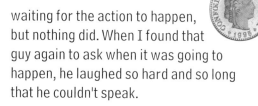

Do you know what happened the first time I went shopping?

I bet it was something funny. Tell me about it.

The first day we arrived, my mom asked me if I could go to the shop next door for some groceries. She gave me a list and some funny money. At first my dad wanted to come with me because he said I was too young to go on my own the first time. That made me really mad. I'm 10 years old and I can surely shop for a few simple things. So they let me go.

I had no trouble finding the milk because 'Milch lait latte' was written on it. But I couldn't find Swiss rolls or Swiss steaks even when I asked a guy who was stacking up cans by a big sign that said 'Aktion'. I stayed around a while

waiting for the action to happen, but nothing did. When I found that guy again to ask when it was going to happen, he laughed so hard and so long that he couldn't speak.

There was also a 'Tageshit' by a stack of bags of noodles but I thought that was a bad word so they couldn't be good. I found so many kinds of muesli in bags, not boxes, that I wasn't sure if it was really muesli or maybe hamster food. And we don't have a hamster yet.

I found all kinds of funny things that I'd never seen before. They showed me where the mustard was, but it was in a tube like toothpaste and I thought YUCK, we can't eat that.

Weight

1 kilogram [kg] = 1,000 grams [g]

1 gram [g] = 0.035 oz
1 kilogram [kg] = 2.205 lb
1 kilogram [kg] = 0.1575 stone

There were lots of things with English names — fresh and fit, quick, soup, low-fat, lifestyle, Flair, Cool Aspirations, Sun Look, Punch, Everyday, and lots of things with 'free' written on them but there was also a price tag so I didn't trust that.

In the end I came home with just the carton of milk. My dad said I told you so, then went to do it himself.

Dad came back an hour later with a big bag filled with Quick Soup cartons saying 'Now I know what you mean.' He had stood for ages at the checkout but

nobody packed up the pile of quick soup cartons. He looked around and noticed that people brought their own bags. He didn't know how to ask for it, so he tried to stack up all the carton cups but dropped them and they rolled everywhere. Every-body was laughing and they gave him a bag.

Dad and Mom started arguing because he said from now on she had to do the shopping. He said 'Shopping in a foreign country makes you feel like you just entered kindergarten!'

Note:
'Swiss rolls' and 'Swiss steaks' are not found in Switzerland (see Misunderstandings on page 39).
Products often have ingredients given on the package in three languages, but not necessarily in English.
'Aktion' means 'sale' and 'Tageshit' means daily special. Mustard, mayonnaise and some breadspreads come in tubes. 'Zuckerfrei' means suger-free. Usually you take your own bag when shopping for groceries, but if you ask, you can also buy one for a small fee.

Volume
1 liter [l] = 10 deciliter [dl]
1 deciliter [dl] = 10 centiliter [cl]

Volume [UK]
1 milliliter [ml] = 0.00176 pt
1 liter [l] = 35.1950 fl oz
1 liter [l] = 1.7598 pt = 0.22 gal

Volume [US]
1 milliliter [ml] = 0.002 11 pt
1 liter [l] = 33.8140 fl oz
1 liter [l] = 2.1134 pt = 0.26 gal

Living in the countryside

Compare the ways of living in the country and the city. Match the pictures on these pages and see the answers below.

Solution: 1E, 2D, 3G, 4C, 5A, 6B, 7F

Living in the city

Festivities

Carnival in Basel (Fasnacht)

Imagine getting up during a winter night to go to a city festival that begins at 4 o'clock in the morning! And surprise! When you get to town, every street, square and lane is packed full of people. There are thousands of beautifully costumed figures, some alone and some in big groups. Street lights are turned off, so most of these figures have lanterns on their heads. They meander through the crowds playing lovely tunes on their piccolos and precise rhythms on their drums behind huge, brightly-lit lanterns covered in artistic cartoons. That's only the beginning of this annual three-day festival. For kids, the best time is Tuesday afternoon. You've got to see it to believe it! You'll find beautiful and outlandish creatures parading all over town. You can't miss enjoying wagons loaded with rambunctious 'Waggis' (a traditional Fasnacht figure) who shower crowds with 'Räppli' (confetti) and toss away candy, flowers and oranges. They love playing tricks on you. (www. fasnacht.ch)

Tuesday afternoon at the Basel Fasnacht you'll see whole families dressed up and playing music.

This young Waggis is harmless, but if you see an adult dressed like this, watch out! They like to play tricks on you, (but afterwards they give you a treat!)

Carnival in Lucerne (Fasnacht)

The exact date of Fasnacht varies each year according to the phase of the moon. In Lucerne it begins with a very loud canon shot at 5 am on 'Schmutziger Donnerstag' (Dirty Thursday). Dress warmly and don't worry about being sleepy at that early hour. The town is full of the crazy sounds and rhythms of the 'Guuggenmusigen' – bands of mostly trumpet and trombone players in wild, colorful, and sometimes frightening costumes. Children from ages 3 to 99 love to dress up in wild costumes and make noise in any imaginable way during the parades on the afternoons of Dirty Thursday and 'Güdis-Mäntig' (Fat Monday). (www.luzerner-fasnacht.ch)

At the Lucerne Fasnacht make your costumes wild and your music loud.

'Räbechilbi' in Richterswil, a town on the Lake of Zurich,
6 pm on the second Saturday in November

*Ich gaa mit myner Latärne
und myni Laterne mit mir.
Am Himmel lüüchted d Stärne,
da unde lüüchted mir.
De Güggel chräät und d Chatz miaut.
Eh, eh, eh, la pimmel, la pimmel, la pumm.*

'Räbeliechtli-Umzug'
(rutabaga lantern parade) in Richterswil

Cutting and carving a hard 'Räbe' (rutabaga or swede) is not so easy. First you have to spoon out the hard center, then carefully cut out designs on the outside. Families and whole communities make these lanterns for a festival with a long tradition. In Richterswil and some other communities, when it is dark and the town's lights go out at 6 pm, about 1,200 children and adults parade with their 'Räbeliechtli' through the streets. (www.vvrs.ch).
They sing a lovely song:

*I'm walking with my lantern,
and my lantern is walking with me.
The stars are shining high above
and we're what's shining down here.
The rooster crows, the cat meows,
je, je, je, la pimmel, la pimmel la pumm.*

Escalade in Geneva

'Fête des vendanges'
in French-speaking Switzerland

This is a two-day festival that takes place in villages and towns all over the French-speaking region. Wine-growers and villagers celebrate the grape harvest with processions and colorful floats making fun of local and international events. School children also take part in the events and enjoy the fun fairs.

'Escalade' in Geneva

The 'Escalade' festival is held in Geneva at the weekend closest to the night of December 11-12. The Genevans commemorate being able to protect themselves from attacks by the troops of the Duke of Savoy in 1602. As the story goes, quick-witted Mother Royaume poured a cauldron of boiling vegetable soup on the enemies pushing their way under her window through the street, which caused them to turn back.

This victory is celebrated every year in the form of a costumed re-enactment parade and costumed children singing for money. Children who are not fond of vegetable soup will delight in finding cauldrons made of chocolate and filled with marzipan vegetables throughout Geneva. (www.compagniede1602.ch)

Festivities

'Trychle' procession in Küssnacht am Rigi

Bells, bells, bells! Swiss people love them! They ring from church steeples, from around cows' and goats' necks (even from horses' necks in a few places in the Jura). Especially in central and northeast Switzerland, people of all ages participate in winter festivities that call for a lot of noise from bells that are carried by people. The loud, deep ringing sound can be scary and mysterious. It comes from processions of 'Trychler' marching around with their huge and heavy tin cowbells strapped around their waists. You'll see hundreds of them parading every year on December 5 in Küssnacht am Rigi.

Hundreds of 'Trychler' parading through Küssnacht am Rigi at the Chlausjagen festivities each year on December 5.

Boys and bells. What a noise!

In Appenzell the bells are particularly decorative.

'Geisle-chlöpfe' (whip cracking competition)

Another old custom is 'Geisle-chlöpfe' – swirling a large and long whip, then suddenly changing the direction which causes the whip to make a very loud sound. In some places in the canton of Lucerne and in the Haslital near Meiringen, you'll hear these loud popping noises and see boys and men cracking whips in the center of villages to attract attention. On dark winter evenings, it's very scary. That's what it is supposed to be, as long ago people believed that this noise would scare away evil spirits. Today it is done as a tradition and just for fun.

Another way to make a lot of noise is by practising whip-cracking for the 'Chlausjagen' festivities.

'Sächsilüte' in Zurich'

'Sächsilüte' is a spring festival in the city of Zurich to drive away winter spirits. The day before, on a Sunday afternoon, children parade the streets in traditional and historical costumes. There's no school in Zurich on Monday and in the afternoon there are colorful parades of guild members, many on horses, also in costume.

Everybody is waiting for the 'Böög' to explode to see if the summer weather will be good.

The highlight of the festival is on Monday at 6 pm on the Sechseläuten-Wiese where a huge bonfire topped by a three-meter tall 'Böög' (which looks like a strange snowman) is set on fire. The Böög's head is stuffed with explosives.

If the fire causes the head to explode soon, it will be a beautiful summer. The longer it takes for the head of the Böög to explode, the more likely it is that the summer will be cold and rainy.

'Knabenschiessen' in Zurich

'Knabenschiessen' also takes place in Zurich on a Monday early in autumn and is a most unusual festival. Translated it means 'boys' shooting' but nowadays girls participate too and have even won the event several times. About 5,000 eight- to fifteen-year-old boys and girls compete in shooting at targets to become the Shooting King or Queen.

Several hundred years ago, at the age of 14 young men were expected to defend the city and this competition was a way of proving one's sharpshooting skills.

Schools are closed all day and there is a 'Chilbi' — a party with lots of rides, Ferris wheels, bumper cars and wild turn-upside-down rides.

49

Winter holidays

Kids arriving the first time in Switzerland late in the year often get a bit confused about all the different Santas and the many customs and traditions during the Christmas season.

On each of the four Sundays before Christmas, many families light a new candle on their Advent wreath.

On December 5, 'Chlausjagen' is held in many places in Central Switzerland (see page 48), in other areas on December 6. St. Nicholas and his assistant (who some people believe come from the Black Forest) visit children to hear them recite verses and remind them of the naughty and nice things they might have done during the year.

In the French-speaking region, people also celebrate St. Nicholas on December 6. St. Nicholas arrives on a donkey early in the evening and is accompanied by Père Fouettard, who is dressed in black and pretends to hit naughty children. Small children get very excited.

Most Swiss families wait until Christmas Eve to decorate their Christmas tree and then, (surprise, surprise) it has real candles burning on it! And ornaments made of real chocolate!

By the time Christmas arrives, these new kids get completely mixed up because they hear that gifts are brought by the 'Christkind' (German), 'Le petit Jésus' (French) or 'Gesù Bambino' (Italian). And a lot of their international friends are convinced that the gifts are from good ole Santa Claus, who is also seen a lot around the country.

Christmas tree in Lucerne

Visits from St. Nicholas used to be a rather upsetting experience, as this picture from the 1950s shows.

Along with nuts and chocolates, you might find a gingerbread cookie like this in the bag St. Nicholas gives you on December 6.

'Grittibänz', a bun kids like to eat on December 6.

You never know when you see a Santa in a shop if maybe he is the real Santa.

There is not one particular dish that everyone has at Christmas celebrations. But there are many traditional cookies that are exchanged as gifts and that are fun to make.

'Schlitteda' in Silvaplana

Chanukah, the Jewish festival of lights, is also celebrated at this time of the year with the holiday menorah. It has nine candles, one for each night of Chanukah. The ninth is used to light the other candles. During Chanukah children like to play Dreidel, a game where you spin a four-sided top with a Hebrew letter on each side.

Everyone is busy at this time of year with parties, making gifts, singing Christmas songs, listening to fairy tales being told in special places (like in some cities in special trams reserved for children).

This is the time that everybody heads for the mountains to enjoy the snow and go skiing, sledding, or ice-skating. Even without doing any of these sports, it's fun just to build a snowman or an igloo or snow castle and to have snowball fights.

Between Christmas and the New Year there are noisy processions of 'Trychler' (see also page 48) in the villages of the Hasliberg and Haslital and in Meiringen.

Is this St. Nick for real? Or is it Santa? What happened to the sleigh? Is he hurrying to get back to the Black Forest or to the North Pole? Or did he forget a surprise for someone? Where did he learn to ski like that? Watch out! He's fast!

On New Year's Eve lots of kids get to stay up until midnight to celebrate the New Year with their families, often with some fireworks.

January 6 is Three Kings Day (Epiphany). It's your chance to be King or Queen for the day if you happen to get the bun on the Three Kings Cake with the hidden toy king in it.

On Three Kings Day in the Lötschental in the canton of Valais, young men costumed as kings prance around on hobby horses. In Schwyz there are whip-cracking competitions and processions of people in Japanese-style costumes. In the canton of Ticino, 'La Befana' puts sweets in the stockings children have hung up for her. Kids in the French-speaking part look out for Chauche-vieille.

The New Year celebrations in Urnäsch (Appenzell O-Rh.) are on January 13, the date of the New Year according to the old Julian calendar. 'Beautiful ', 'ugly ', and 'forest Kläuse' go around in their elaborate costumes and headdresses to spread New Year's greetings.

Spring and summer holidays

Weeks before Easter you'll find lots of colorful Easter decorations, chocolate bunnies, eggs and other goodies in shops. Good Friday and Easter Monday are holidays (no school!), which means many families use these days for travelling. Somehow the Easter Bunny is always able to keep up with them. On Easter Sunday morning, kids go looking for the colorful eggs the Easter Bunny hid for them during the night.

Those who stay at home also have lots of fun coloring eggs, baking 'Osterfladen' (a pie made of semolina or rice with lemon, eggs, raisins, and cream). Some communities have egg races, Easter processions and Biblical Passion Plays.

Ascension Day and Whit Monday are also holidays.

Easter Bunny buns are found at all bakeries and it's fun to bake your own.

Do Easter eggs grow on trees?

The Easter Bunny has many disguises.

What could be nicer than a sunny spring day on a mountain!

August 1: the Swiss National Day

Late in the evening on August 1, the best place to be is up on a hilltop with a view of a valley or of a city celebrating Switzerland's anniversary of the oath taken in 1291. You'll see lots of bonfires in the hills and fireworks sparkling in all directions. Communities everywhere hold celebrations. You can join parades of children with their candle-lit lanterns and enjoy the noise and sparkles of your own fireworks with your family.

August 1 is a national holiday, so there's no school and offices and shops are closed.

In some places (Basel, for example), August 1 is a holiday but it's celebrated the evening before on July 31, so don't miss it!

The oath taken in 1291 is celebrated on August 1.

Kids enjoy staying up late and carrying candle-lit lanterns around on August 1.

Being square, the Swiss flag is ideal for the tradition of flag-throwing.

53

Sports and games in winter

In winter when the sun shines
All kids head for the hills
To find endless new ways
to enjoy wild thrills.

When skies turn gray and cloudy
and a freezing cold wind blows
You just gotta dress warmer
As every Swiss kid knows.

Sports and games in summer

In summer when the sun shines
Kids simply can't be stopped
From sharing fun and games
'Til the sun's finally plopped.

When the Föhn's blown away,
Leaving hills swept with rain,
There's still lots of games to play
So Swiss kids can't complain.

Sports, games and fun

Summer is fun. There are many different outdoor activities you can do when the weather is good: hiking, climbing, cycling, swimming, skating, playing frisbee, badminton, volleyball or any other ball game, jumping hopscotch or splashing in the nearest pool or lake.

Water slide in Reiden, canton Lucerne

Swimming at the Lake of Lauerz with a view of Mount Mythen

Swiss kids love roasting 'Cervelat' outdoors over an open fire.

'Jass' is a popular Swiss card game and its rules can be found in English at www.pagat.com/jass/swjass.html.

How to decide who is 'out'.

Eeny, meeny, miny, moe
Catch a tiger by the toe
If he hollers let him go,
Eeny, meeny, miny, moe.

(in Swiss dialect)

Aa zellä Böllä schellä
d Chatz gaat uf Wallisellä
chunt 'si wider häi
hät si chrumi Bei
piff paff puff
und du bisch ehr und
redlich duss.

(in French)

Am stram gram
Pique et pique et colegram
Bourg et bourg et ratatam
Am stram gram
Pique dame!

'Schwingen' – Swiss wrestling

'Schwingen'
is the Swiss version of
wrestling related to judo.
Opponents first shake
hands, then grip each
other's special pants and
wrestle until one of them is
on his back in the sawdust
or the time for the round
expires. One hand always
holds the opponent's
special pants. The winner
always brushes the saw-
dust off the loser's back and
they shake hands again.

And the greatest sport
of all: sleeping and dreaming
under a fluffy feather comforter.

How do people live?

Houses in Switzerland look different and vary in size depending on when and where they were built. In earlier times, people in the countryside or up in the moutains used to build houses of wood as that building material was cheap and readily available. In the cities houses were usually built of stone.

Goats living on the balcony of a chalet in Guarda
(canton of Grisons)

Farmhouse in the canton of Appenzell

Block of apartments in Zurich

When you go to small villages in the countryside you often find a mixture of old wooden farmhouses, modern detached or semi-detached houses, and blocks of apartments.

Oberstammheim-Hüttwilersee, canton Zurich

Residential area in Reinach, Basel-Landschaft

For an exciting adventure to learn how people all over Switzerland used to live, go to the open-air musem in Ballenberg near Brienz. You won't regret it!

Blocks of apartments in Adligenswil near Lucerne

Even though it looks like there are houses just about everywhere where you travel except in the mountains or remote areas, the majority of people in Switzerland live in apartments with a small balcony.

Traditional Swiss food
Breakfast, lunch and dinner

'Birchermüesli'

'Birchermüesli' (cereals, yoghurt, fresh fruits) is part of a traditional Swiss breakfast but can be eaten at any time of the day.

'Bernerplatte'

'Bernerplatte', a specialty of the canton of Berne, is a plate of ham, sausage, smoked pork, sauerkraut, beans, and potatoes.

Bread

Bread comes in all shapes, sizes and tastes (dark, wholemeal, white). On Sunday people usually eat 'Zopf', a white plaited bread, for breakfast.

'Risotto'

'Risotto', a creamy rice dish from the canton of Ticino, comes in many flavors.

Cheese plate

You'll be amazed to find so many different types of cheese, not only the one with holes.

'Pizokel'

'Pizokel', home-baked spinach dumplings, are a culinary delight of the Grisons region.

'Bündnerteller'

Another specialty from the canton of Grisons is the 'Bündnerteller', a plate of salami, different kinds of dried meat, cheese and pickled gherkins.

Raclette (literally 'scraped cheese')

'Raclette' is a popular dish of melted cheese served with boiled potatoes, gherkins and pickled onions.

How to prepare your Swiss-style sausage before grilling it over the open fire

Bring your 'Cervelat' or 'Bratwurst', a popular sausage you can buy in any grocery store.

Cut a deep cross into each end of the sausage with your Swiss army knife or any other sharp knife.

Find a stick, sharpen one end with your knife and put the sausage on the tip.

Roast your sausage over the fire until it's brown and the divided ends curve. Get your chips, bread, mustard or ketchup, tomatoes, cucumber, etc.

Now you can enjoy your sausage.

'En Guete!'

Desserts

Fruit pies, this one is with plums

The Swiss love desserts and baked goods. Wherever you go, you can choose from a huge selection of sweets, ranging from pies, 'Birnenbrot' (loaf-shaped cake filled with a mass of pear, apple, plums, figs, nuts, etc.), carrot cake to 'Vermicelles' (made of chestnuts, but looks like a pile of long worms – children either love it or hate it).

'Caramelchöpfli' (crème caramel)

'Birnenbrot'

Chocolate

Strawberry tart

'Vermicelles'

And last but not least, don't forget to taste Swiss chocolate – it comes in different flavors and shapes. Mind you, you can't only eat chocolate, you can also drink it hot. It's delicious!

'Rüeblichueche' (carrot cake)

Have you ever tried fondue? If not, you need to taste the most famous Swiss dish. If you don't like cheese, try one of the meat fondues. There's also a chocolate version for those who have a sweet tooth. But don't eat it all, it's really rich.

How do people get around?

STOP! DON'T WALK! Wait until the light turns green.

Look left, right, left before crossing the road. Now you can cross.

We wear our bright orange vests so that we are seen easily when walking to and from school.

Maybe Michael Schumacher drives his kids to school with his racing car?

Anyway, most kids have to run to school because they are late.

Length

1 centimeter [cm] = 0.3937 in
1 meter [m] = 3.2808 ft
1 meter [m] = 1.0936 yd
1 kilometer [km] = 0.6214 miles

What do children read?

Oh, I completely forgot about it. It's the annual 'Children's Storytelling Event'.

What's happening over there?

Are they also reading Heidi to the kids?

Franz Hohler reading to some of his many fans

I guess so. They always read the famous ones. Let's go over there and have a look! Hey! That's Franz Hohler! You'll love him!

Wait a second! "... written by René Goscinny and illustrated by Albert Uderzo." Yes, of course those two famous French guys ... !

Asterix and Obelix take you on an adventure to Switzerland. Don't miss out on this action-packed, funny and really enjoyable trip.

Asterix in Switzerland by René Goscinny and Albert Uderzo

Tschipo dreams a lot and his dreams are often pretty wild. When he wakes up in the morning there are things he just dreamt about in his room. But the real adventure begins when Tschipo wakes up on an island after having dreamed of being on one.

Tschipo by Franz Hohler

Excusez-moi, puis-je vous déranger?

Mi scusi, posso disturbarla?

Stgisai, As poss jau disturbar?

Es-tu nouveau/nouvelle ici?

Sei nuovo/a qui?

Es ti nov/a qua?

C'est vraiment un bon jeu, ne trouves-tu pas?

È veramente un bel gioco, non trovi?

Quai è in grondius gieu, navair?

Est-ce que je peux aussi jouer?

Posso giocare anch'io?

Astg jau giugar cun vus?

Tu as l'air fâché. C'est-il passé
        quelque chose?

Hai l'aria contrariata; ti è successo
        qualcosa?

Ti fas ina trista tschera. Èsi schabegià
        insatge?

As-tu besoin d'aide?

Hai bisogno d'aiuto?

Poss jau gidar tai?

As-tu du plaisir?

Ti diverti?

Has plaschair?

Est-ce que çà te ferait quelque chose?

Ti dispiacerebbe (fare qualcosa) per me?

Pudessas ti (far insatge) ... per mai?

Are you new here?

Bist du neu hier?

Bisch neu da?

Excuse me, may I disturb you??

Entschuldigung, darf ich Sie stören?

Entschuldigung, dörf ich Sie schtöre?

Yes, I've just arrived and I can't find the ...

Ja, ich bin eben erst angekommen und kann ... nicht finden.

Ja, ich bi grad acho und chan ... nöd finde.

It's a great game, isn't it?

Ist doch ein tolles Spiel, nicht wahr?

Isch doch es super Schpiel, oder?

May I help you?

Kann ich dir helfen?

Chan ich dir hälfe?

You look upset! Is something wrong?

Du siehst aufgeregt aus. Ist etwas passiert?

Du gsehsch ufgregt us. Isch öppis passiert?

Would you mind ... (doing something) ... for me?

Würde es dir etwas ausmachen, ... ?

Würds dir öppis usmache, ...?

Having fun?

Hast du Spass?

Häsch es luschtig?

I've been waiting an hour for you!

Ich warte nun schon eine Stunde auf dich!

Jetzt wart ich scho ä ganzi Stund uf dich!

I hope you are feeling better.

Ich hoffe, dir geht es wieder besser.

Hoffentlich gahts der wieder besser.

Quick! I need your help!

Schnell! Ich brauche deine Hilfe!

Schnäll! Ich bruche dini Hilf!

Could I borrow … (something) … ?

Darf ich … (etwas) … ausleihen?

Chan ich … (öppis) … churz uslehne?

Do you want to play/eat with me?

Willst Du mit mir spielen/essen?

Wetsch mit mir schpile/ässe?

YOU MUST BE JOKING!

DU MACHST WOHL WITZE!

DU MACHSCH WOHL EN WITZ!

May I ask you something?

Darf ich dich etwas fragen?

Dörf ich dich öppis froge?

YOU MUST BE JOKING!

DU MACHST WOHL WITZE!

DU MACHSCH WOHL EN WITZ!

J'espère que tu vas de nouveau mieux.

Spero che ti senti meglio.

Jau sper che ti ta sentias puspè meglier.

Je t'attends déjà depuis une heure.

È già un'ora che ti aspetto!

Jau spetg gia dapi in'ura sin tai!

Est-ce que j'ose emprunter … ?

Potresti prestarm … ?

Astg jau emprestar … ?

Vite! J'ai besoin de ton aide!

Fai presto, ho bisogno del tuo aiuto!

Spert, jau dovrel tes agid!

Tu racontes des blagues!

Stai scherzando!

Ti fas sgnoccas!

Veux-tu jouer/manger avec moi?

Vuoi giocare/mangiare con me?

Vuls ti giugar/mangiar cun mai?

Tu racontes des blagues!

Stai scherzando!

Ti fas sgnoccas!

Est-ce que je peux te demander quelque chose?

Posso domandarti una cosa?

Astg jau dumandar tai insatge?

Pardon, qu'as-tu dit?

Scusa, come hai detto?

Stgisa, tge has ditig?

Je regrette mais mon bus avait du retard.

Mi dispiace, ma il mio bus ha fatto ritardo.

Jau stun mal, mes bus ha gì retard.

Oui, je cherche le rayon des jouets.

Sì, sto cercando il reparto giocattoli.

Gea, jau tschertg la partiziun da termagls.

Que s'est-il passé?

Cos'è successo?

Tge è schabegià?

Eeeeeeee, je ne suis pas sûr.

Hmmm, non ne sono sicuro.

Hmmm, jau na sun betg segir/segira.

Excuse-moi je t'en prie, c'était une erreur.

Ti prego scusami, c'è stato un errore.

Perstgisa, quai è stà in sbagl!

Pas de quoi, bien sûr je …

Macchè, certamente io …

Pertge dumondas ti?

Pourquoi demandes-tu?

Perché chiedi?

Pertge dumondas ti?

I'm awfully sorry. My bus was late.

Es tut mir leid, aber mein Bus war verspätet.

Es tut mer leid, aber min Bus isch zspat cho.

Could you say that again?

Wie bitte, was hast du gesagt?

Was häsch gseit?

What happened?

Was ist passiert?

Was isch passiert?

Yes, I'm looking for the toy department.

Ja, ich suche die Spielzeugabteilung.

Ja, ich suäch d'Spielzügabteilig.

I'm sorry, it was an accident!

Entschuldige bitte, es war ein Missgeschick!

Entschuldigung, es isch äs Missgschick gsi!

Mmmmmmmm, I'm not sure.

Mmmmmm, ich bin nicht sicher.

Mmmmmm, ich bin nöd sicher.

Why do you ask?

Weshalb fragst du?

Warum frögsch?

That's no problem! Of course I'll …

Keine Ursache! Natürlich werde ich …

Keis Problem! Sicher wird ich …

Non, je cherche les toilettes.

No, sto cercando la toilette.

Na, jau tschertg las tualettas.

Rien de grave, j'arrive juste de chez le dentiste.

Niente di grave, sono giusto di ritorno dal dentista.

I n'è nagut nausch, jau vegn gist dal dentist.

Oui, je viens juste d'arriver et ne peux trouver …

Sì, sono appena arrivato e non riesco a trovare …

Gea, jau sun gist arrivà/-ada, ed jau na chat betg …

Bien sûr que j'aimerais ça.

Ma certo che ti piacerà.

Cler che quai ma plaschess.

Sans doute.

Senza dubbio!

Senza dubi!

Pardon?

Come?

Co?

Oui, çà serait chouette.

Sì, questo sarebbe divertente.

Gea, quai fiss grondius!

J'ai de bonnes/mauvaises nouvelles.

Ho delle buone/nuove notizie.

Jau hai nauschas/bunas novas.

It's nothing really. I just got home from the dentist.

Nichts Schlimmes, ich komme gerade vom Zahnarzt.

Nüt Schlimms, ich chum grad vom Zahnarzt.

No, I'm looking for the boys'/girls' room.

Nein, ich suche das Klo.

Nei, ich suächs WC.

Certainly, I'd like that.

Natürlich würde mir das gefallen.

Natürlich würd mir das gfalle.

Yes, I've just arrived and I can't find the …

Ja, ich bin eben erst angekommen und kann … nicht finden.

Ja, ich bi grad acho und chan … nöd finde.

I beg your pardon!

Wie bitte?

Wiä bitte?

There's no doubt about it!

Zweifelsohne!

Kei Zwiifel!

I've got bad/good news.

Ich habe schlechte/gute Nachrichten.

Ich ha schlächti/guäti Neuikeitä.

Yes, that would be fun.

Ja, das würde Spass machen.

Ja, das wär schpassig.

For full instructions see pages 124-125.

I like this one!

Heidi, an orphan, is sent to live with her grumpy grandfather in the Alps. She becomes very fond of the old man and the simple but peaceful life in the mountains. It comes as quite as shock when all of a sudden she is taken to a big city where she is to keep company to a sick, but very sweet girl.

Heidi by Johanna Spyri

The Rainbow Fish by Marcus Pfister

I still like this one.

Ursli does not want to be the boy with the smallest bell at the spring festival's procession. So he decides to venture to his family's hut up in the mountains to get the big cowbell.

A Bell for Ursli by Selina Chönz and Alois Cariget

The Rainbow Fish is the most beautiful fish in the entire ocean. He has iridescent scales and is not only very proud of them, but also vain and selfish. Since he would never dream of sharing his scales with other fish, he does not have many friends, but that'll soon change.

Marta is a cow, but not an ordinary one. She is orange and loves to go on adventurous trips. This time she is taking a trip to find the country of hot-air balloons.

Marta au pays des montgolfières by Germano Zullo and Albertine

Topino diventa grande by Bruna Martinelli, Sergio Simona

Titeuf, the comic figure with an egg-shaped head and an ostrich feather on it, is a typical, curious, loud-mouthed, and provocative teenager who wants to explore and understand the adult world, but isn't always able to.

Titeuf is cool! Didn't you say he is from the French-speaking part of Switzerland? Let's go meet him!

Topino is a small and shy mouse that decides to find the queen of the mice. On her adventurous trip she faces many dangerous situations, makes new friends and learns what it means to enjoy life.

Titeuf by Zep

Helikopter (Helicopter)

Un - der - halb vom Mat - ter - horn isch öp - pis pas - siert, Es
Just be - low the Mat - ter - horn there's some - thing gone wrong, An

gaht um Lä - be o - der Tod, es pres - siert. Es
ac - ci - dent, it's life or death; please please rush a - long, For

isch öp - per ab - gschtürzt und hät sich ver - letzt, dä sött drin - gend zum Tok - ter
some - one has fal - len and ta - ken a blow, and if he'll sur - vive, we

und zwar jetzt. Änd - lich chunnt de Ret - tigs - he - li - kop - ter,
really don't know. Just in time the res - cue he - li - cop - ter

flüügt mit Voll - gas uf eus zue Zäh Me - ter ü - ber eus-
speeds to - wards us so we shout Ten met - ers o - ver our

ne Chöpf schtoppt er, und mit de Seil - win - de ziend's eus ue.
heads it ho - vers, drops us a line and then pulls us out.

2. Mängisch träumi Sache, wo sich nöd jede getraut
Zum Biischpiil hani mal am König sini Chrone klaut
Ich riite gschnäll devo demit uf mim schwarze Hängscht
Am König sini Riiter holed uf, ich han Angscht!

3. D'Namitäg bim Lehrer Pfischter sind e Qual
Langwiiligi Drüüegg zeichne mit em Lineal
Uf de Millimeter gnau, als chäm's druffa
Da würd me sich am liebschte us
De Schtund entfüehre lah.

2. Sometimes I dream dreams that other
    dreamers dread.
There was a time I dreamt I stole a king's
    crown from his head,
Raced off on my black horse with knights in pursuit,
Then I jumped off a cliff with my parachute.

3. Afternoons with teacher Pfister are such a bore,
Drawing perfect triangles and squares by the score,
They must be exact — oh! it's driving me crazy,
Please take me away and let me be lazy.

Music: Schtärneföifi, lyrics: Boni Koller
www.schtaerne5i.ch

66

Le vieux chalet (The Old Chalet)

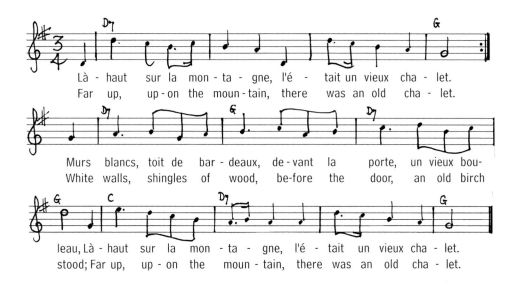

Là - haut sur la mon - ta - gne, l'é - tait un vieux cha - let.
Far up, up - on the moun - tain, there was an old cha - let.

Murs blancs, toit de bar - deaux, de - vant la porte, un vieux bou-
White walls, shingles of wood, be - fore the door, an old birch

leau, Là - haut sur la mon - ta - gne, l'é - tait un vieux cha - let.
stood; Far up, up - on the moun - tain, there was an old cha - let.

2. Là-haut sur la montagne, croula le vieux chalet.
La neige et les rochers s'étaient unis pour l'arracher
Là-haut sur la montagne, croula le vieux chalet.

3. Là-haut sur la montagne, quand Jean vint au chalet.
Pleura de tout son coeur sur les débris de son bonheur
Là-haut sur la montagne, quand Jean vint au chalet.

4. Là-haut sur la montagne, l'est un nouveau chalet.
Car Jean d'un coeur vaillant l'a reconstruit plus beau qu'avant
Là-haut sur la montagne, l'est un nouveau chalet.

2. Far up, upon the mountain, there fell the old chalet.
The snow and rocks around, together they did bring it down.
Far up, upon the mountain, there fell the old chalet.

3. Far up, upon the mountain, when John saw the old chalet.
With all his heart he cried o'er what misfortune did betide.
Far up, upon the mountain, John mourned his old chalet.

4. Far up, upon the mountain, there is a new chalet
For John with heart so true, rebuilt it better than he knew.
Far up, upon the mountain, there is a new chalet.

Composed by Abbé Joseph Bovet in 1911,
property of Editions Foetisch, Lausanne.

67

L'inverno è passato (The Winter now is over)

L'in-ver-no l'è pas-sa- to, l'a-pri-le non c'è più, è rit-or-na-to il
The win-ter now is o-ver, and A-pril rains are past; I know I heard this

mag-gio col can - to del cu- cù. Cu - cù Cu - cù l'a-
morn- ing the cu-ckoo's song at last. Cu - ckoo Cu - ckoo Oh,

pri-le non c'è più; è ri - tor-nato il mag - gio col can -to del cu-
can't you hear it too? I know I heard this morn - ing the cu -ckoo's song at

cù. Cu - cù Cu - cù, l'a - pri-le non c'è più; è
last. Cu - ckoo Cu - ckoo Oh, can't you hear it too? I

rit - or-nato il mag - gio col can - to del cu - cù.
know I heard this morn - ing the cu -ckoo's song at last.

2. Lassù per le montagne
la neve non c'è più,
comincia a fare il nido
il povero cucù.
Cucù cucù.
la neve …

2. The sun on ev'ry mountain
has melted winter's snow;
The birds build in the treetops
the cuckoo's call they know.
Cuckoo cuckoo
I know …

3.La bella alla finestra
la guarda in su e in giù,
l'aspetta il fidanzato
al canto del cucù.
Cucù cucù,
la guarda …

3. I sit beside my window,
I feel the cuckoo's spell;
'Tis May, and sure my sweeheart
must hear the song as well.
Cuckoo cuckoo
I know …

La chanzun dal sulai (The Song about the Sun)

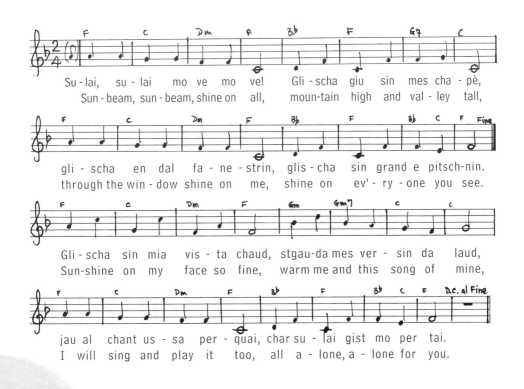

Su - lai, su - lai mo ve mo ve! Gli - scha giu sin mes cha - pè,
Sun - beam, sun - beam, shine on all, moun-tain high and val - ley tall,

gli - scha en dal fa - ne - strin, glis - cha sin grand e pitsch-nin.
through the win - dow shine on me, shine on ev' - ry - one you see.

Gli - scha sin mia vis - ta chaud, stgau-da mes ver - sin da laud,
Sun-shine on my face so fine, warm me and this song of mine,

jau al chant us - sa per - quai, char su - lai gist mo per tai.
I will sing and play it too, all a - lone, a - lone for you.

(in Italian)
Sole, sole, la tua scintilla
sopra la mia casa brilla,
brilla oggi su di me,
ed io canterò per te.

(in French)
Soleil soleil tout là-haut
Toi qui brille sur mon chapeau
par la fenêtre brille sur moi
et je chanterai pour toi.

(in Swiss German)
Schiin mer warm und hell ins Gsicht,
wärm mi uf und das Gedicht,
wo ni do am Singe bi,
isch defür allei für di.

(in German)
Sonne Sonne Sonnenstrahl
leuchte über Berg und Tal
leuchte mir zum Fenster rein
schein' auf alle gross und klein
scheine hell auf mein Gesicht
Wärme mich und mein Gedicht
Sonne Sonne singe ich
ganz allein, allein für dich.

Music by Linard Bardill.
Lyrics by Lorenz Pauli.

What about schools?

In Germany babies come from the stork.

In France I'm not so sure but I think it's got something to do with men and women.

I don't know how it's done in Switzerland, but I'm sure it's different in every canton.

26 cantons = 26 educational systems

Kindergarten is usually for two years, then regardless of whether you are a boy or a girl and whatever country you come from and whatever religion you have, you have to go to school for nine years. Schooling is also provided for disabled people and socially disadvantaged children.

First you go to a primary and then to a lower secondary level. Moving from one level to the next is in some cantons after four, in others after five, and in some others after six years. After completing nine years of school, you do not receive a final diploma. The reports you receive twice a year serve as evidence of your skills and progress.

When you receive the upper secondary level of education you go to a 'high school' called 'Gymnasium', 'Lycée' or 'Liceo' where you can obtain a certificate called the 'Matura' which will entitle you to study at any university in the country.

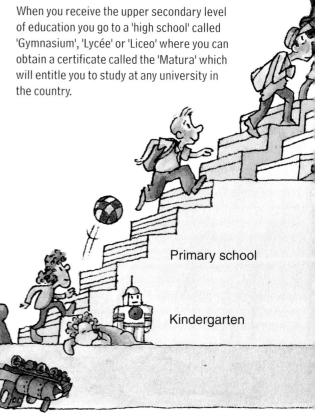

Primary school

Kindergarten

Cantonal
universities,
federal
institutes
of technology

Universities
of applied
sciences
and arts

Gymnasium

Apprenticeship

Upper secondary school

Lower secondary school

A lot of boys and girls get vocational training after their basic nine years of schooling. Having an apprenticeship in an occupation means you will be taught practical skills on the job for several days a week, then get theoretical education the rest of the week at a school.

You get a diploma when you finish your apprenticeship and then you can decide if you want to move on to a higher level of training.

Differences you need to know about

You'll find some decoration on letters of the alphabet and it's a good idea to pay attention to these as you learn a new language.

In German there are two little dots over some letters called an 'Umlaut'. These letters look like this:

ä ö ü

They change the way the letter is pronounced and might also sometimes change the meaning of a word. For example Küche = kitchen, Kuchen = cake, or schön = beautiful, schon = already.

In Switzerland, the extra letter of the German alphabet called the 'Doppel S' is written ss.

28

28

Another thing that might confuse you when listening to people say numbers in German or Swiss German is that they say, for example, for the number twenty-eight 'achtundzwanzig' (8 + 20) and not 'zwanzigundacht' (20 + 8).

In French and Italian there are also sometimes accents and markings over letters like this:

These accents on the letters enable the reader to distinguish between identical sounding words, e.g. a and à, ou and où, du and dû. They may also show that a letter has been dropped, e.g. hospital has become hôpital, castle has become château.

The first floor of a building is not the ground floor like in some countries, but the first floor above the gound floor. The ground floor is called in German 'das Erdgeschoss' or 'das Parterre'.

When addressing letters to people in Switzerland, be sure you put the postal code before the Swiss city (not after it) and put your own address on the back of the envelope and not on the front. The stamp goes on the front at the top right corner. You can stamp it to be sent by 'priority' A-mail (to be delivered in 1 or 2 days) or otherwise by B-mail.

You may find that there are different ways of writing some numbers, especially in handwriting:

Number 1 may be written as **1** or **1** .
Number 7 is handwritten with a cross through it like this **7** .
So be careful you don't mix up your numbers one and seven!

And sometimes the zero will have a line through it to look like this **Ø** .

Some numbers in the French-speaking part of the country are different than they are in France:

70
French = soixante-dix
Swiss French = septante

80
French = quatre-vingts
Swiss French = huitante
(You'll find this in Valais and Vaud
but not in Geneva, the Jura or in Neuchhâtel)

99
French = quatre-vingts-dix-neuf
Swiss French = nonante-neuf

Watch out! When you show with your fingers how many you want of something, remember that your thumb is one as shown below.

one week

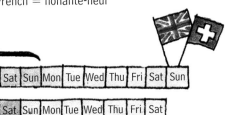

| Mon | Tue | Wed | Thu | Fri | Sat | Sun | Mon | Tue | Wed | Thu | Fri | Sat | Sun |

| Sun | Mon | Tue | Wed | Thu | Fri | Sat | Sun | Mon | Tue | Wed | Thu | Fri | Sat |

one week

Most calendars in Switzerland (and Britain too) show Monday as the first day of the week, whereas in America, Canada and Australia and other countries the first day of the week is Sunday.

School's out!

Usually Wednesday afternoons are school-free. In some places kids go to school on Saturday mornings. School vacation in summer usually lasts five weeks. In some places this begins the first week in July and ends after the first week in August. There is also school vacation for two weeks in autumn, usually around the first two weeks in October. Also in winter there are two weeks when schools close and sometimes school classes go together to ski camps for a week. And of course there is no school on official holidays like Christmas, New Year's Day, Easter, Ascension Day and Whit Monday.

A Rainy Day: a short one-act play
Practise your theatrical skills

[Scene: a shelter on the playgroud. Susy runs for the shelter through the rain to join Angela.]

Angela: Hi Susy. Are you enjoying the rain?

Susy: No! How can you enjoy rain?! I wish I could go back to bed and start this day all over again. I missed going on a trip with some other kids.

Angela: What happened?

Susy: I got up late. Spilled the Bircher-muesli. Couldn't find my backpack. The stupid tram took too long to get to the station. While running to the train, a dog dashed in front of me and I tripped over the leash and fell.

Angela: Did you hurt yourself?

Susy: No, but I landed on my lunch in the backpack and the mustard in my sandwich got all mixed up with the chocolate cake Tommy and I made yesterday to share with the other kids.

When I got to the platform where the kids were meeting, nobody was there! The train was gone. I was only one minute late! **I hate it when trains are on time! I hate it here! Everything is different. The language, the sevens, the weather, the kids. I wanna go back home to the way things used to be ... boohoohoohoo.**

Angela: Oh, poor Susy. Today hasn't been a good day for me either.

Susy: What happened to you?

Angela: Nothing like what happened to you. I've just learned I'm moving away from here, and it makes me very sad because I'd like to stay.

Susy: But you can't move! This is your home! You've always been here.

Angela: No, you haven't noticed but I was a foreigner when I came here too. Like you and Tommy, I had to get used to life here too. It wasn't always easy but you know what? Now I realize that kids here are just as much fun as the kids where I came from, they just do some things differently. Had I always stayed where I came from, I think I would have missed so many good things.

Susy: But don't you miss your old friends?

Angela: Sure I do! We keep in touch. But when I've gone back to see them, they've changed. Lots of things I enjoy here aren't there. It was like seeing 'home' with new eyes. If I had to live there I'd miss so many things that are here and be 'homesick' for here. Here or there, there or here – there's good things in both places.

[Silence, rain, rain, rain]

Angela: Let's read 'Heidi' together. Do you want to take turns reading it out loud?

[As they read it rains harder, then the sun comes out]

Susy: Heidi was unhappy from having to move around too. Would she have been happy had she never left the alp? She would have missed an awful lot.

Angela: I don't know.

Susy: Look how pretty the rain drops are on those leaves! Isn't the sky a pretty color?

Angela: I guess things just always happen as they must.

[Other kids show up]

Kids: Hey, Susy, what happened? Where have you been?

Susy: I missed the train.

Kids: Lucky you! Our picnic was a disaster. We all got wet and muddy and everyone was bored and grumpy. You didn't miss a thing!

Susy: I guess this is my lucky day after all.

Angela: You never know!

How about exciting excursions?

All over the country you can go on some very exciting hikes on adventurous paths that take you up and down steep slopes, sit on mountain peaks, climb down ladders into gorges or, like in this picture at the Trift Glacier in the Bernese Oberland, cross vast spaces on hanging bridges over rivers, glaciers and canyons. There's never a dull moment!

Suspension bridge over the Trift Glacier

Fancy being an artist? The children's museum Creaviva is part of the Paul Klee Center and offers you the opportunity to have a go at art. You can draw, paint, make a craft, act, experience and discover or simply explore Paul Klee's art. If you want to be creative, try that museum. (www.zpk.org)

Children's museum Creaviva in Bern.

Would you like to know more about how people used to travel and communicate and how we might in the future? The Swiss Museum of Transport and Communication is a hands-on museum where you can discover and explore means of transportation and communication in the past, present and future. Young explorers can also experience flying a plane or driving a train in a simulator. If you're too small for that, you can build your own train tracks or spend some time on the Kids Cargo playground. And don't miss the bird's-eye view of Switzerland while taking a short walk across the country. (www.verkehrshaus.ch)

Museum of Transport and Communication in Lucerne

Swissminiatur in Melide

Switzerland is small, but did you know that you can actually visit the country in one day? Swissminiatur in Melide, near Lugano, lets you stroll around and across Switzerland in just a few hours while visiting all the main cities, climbing up the mountains and enjoying the mild, Mediterranean climate. There's also a train that takes you to all the important places. (www.swissminiatur.ch)

The magnificent Castle of Chillon on Lac Léman

There are many furnished castles in Switzerland where the Middle Ages come alive and where you can see how knights and damsels used to live. Running up and down the stairs and exploring the dungeons is exciting and quite an experience. In some castles you can even dress up as knights or damsels. (www.chillon.ch)

Technorama is a science center where you can watch, listen, experiment and find answers to natural phenomena and tricky scientific questions. It's the place to go if you want to know more about science and technology and learn about it in a playful way. Ask your parents to come with you, they can learn a lot too! (www.technorama.ch)

See pages 110-113 for more information on interesting places to visit.

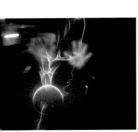

Technorama, the Swiss Science Center in Winterthur

Democracy and parliament

I wanna go play!

What do those people on the billboards advertise?

Nothing, those are all election candidates.

Election candidates???

Yes, candidates running for parliament. Let me explain the political system in this country.

When Switzerland was founded in 1291, it consisted of three regions or what you nowadays call cantons. Over the years, more cantons joined the loose association and eventually its members decided it was time they created a federal state. Finally, in 1848 they founded the modern Swiss Confederation (Confoederatio Helvetica) with a constitution and a federal parliament. Now there are 26 cantons and half-cantons in Switzerland.

Switzerland is a federal state. Unlike many other countries around the world it doesn't have a president or a prime minister but a federal government.

Switzerland is run by:

the Federal Council (executive power), a seven-member cabinet that takes decisions. Each year a cabinet minister is elected president for one calendar year to represent the government in Switzerland and abroad.

You can visit the Parliament Building in Berne. It's an impressive place.

Besides the federal authorities there are also municipal and cantonal authorities that are in charge of local issues like education, church matters, finances and income tax, etc.

the Federal Assembly (legislative power) or parliament. It is divided into two chambers with equal power and each chamber meets for four three-week sessions each year:

The National Council represents the people and has 200 members.

The Council of States represents the cantons. It has 46 members: two representatives of each canton and one of each half-canton.

National Council

Council of States

Votes, initiatives and referenda

The Swiss have their say in politics. Citizens over 18 can elect the parliamentarians (every four years on the penultimate Sunday in October) and vote on changes to the constitution and on new laws (four times a year). But they also have the right to put forward and sign initiatives and referenda.

Popular initiative

If you want to make an amendment to the constitution, you need to make a proposal and collect 100,000 signatures over a period of 18 months.

Referendum

To demand a popular vote on laws passed by legislature, you have to collect 50,000 signatures within 100 days.

Democracy and parliament

Let's go home! I'm hungry, thirsty and bored.

What do you wanna do at home?

Why don't we go to the playground?

We can't do everything at the same time, we need to decide!

I don't know. I can't make up my mind.

We could play computer games or ...

Any other suggestions? So, let's vote!

How do people vote in Switzerland?

Voting takes place about four times a year. Swiss citizens over 18 receive their voting material, including brochures, leaflets and ballot papers, by post. After filling in the ballot papers, they can either return them by post or cast their votes at a polling station on voting day. E-voting and SMS voting are being promoted, but haven't been introduced.

Who wants to go home?

Who wants to go to the playground?

Hey, 2-1 against going to the playground, so let's go home.

What's that map for and why are there only a few green spots?

That's what voting results in Switzerland often look like: everybody votes No except the French-speaking part and Basel.

Yes

No

Dos and don'ts for children

Peter Meier

Give your name
when answering the phone.

Look at people when talking
to them.

Don't drop your piece of bread
into the fondue pot, otherwise
you have to give everybody a
kiss.

Don't chase cows or they may
turn around and chase you!

Be polite

In English you can use 'you' to
address adults and children alike.
In German, French, Italian, and
Romansh, you need to distinguish
between a familiar form for kids
of about the same age and a polite
form for adults:

Form	Familiar	Polite
German	du	Sie
Swiss German	du	Sii
French	tu	Vous
Italian	tu	Lei
Romansh	ti	Vus

Don't shoot apples
off people's heads!

Grüezi Herr Bieri! Hoi Jessica!

Shake hands.

When meeting neighbors or
people you know, greet them
by name.

Good morning Alice and Jim!

Hi Mr. Rüdisüli!

Things that
are forbidden
are usually on
round signs.

Grüezi Salut Ciao

82

Watch out! Danger!

Don't touch nettles! They really burn! If you do, it helps to put cold water on the spot that hurts.

Wear appropriate shoes in the mountains.

Danger signs are triangular!

In spring watch out for frogs and toads on the road!

Don't lick snow off a railing in winter when it's icy!

The 'Züghuusjoggeli'
(The Jester at the Old Arsenal Museum, Solothurn)

The 'Züghuusjoggeli' is the most famous person in the city of Solothurn. One night in the 19th century it's said he hid inside a suit of armour that he assumed belonged to the jester of Charles the Bold, who lived from 1433 - 1477. The 'Züghuusjoggeli' is still hiding there! If you look into his eyes and lift the visor of his helmet, you get a special surprise. He really spits at you!

real size

enlarged tick

Tick bites can make you sick. So make sure your parents check you for ticks after you've been playing in the forest.

Don't even touch this fly agaric ('Fliegenpilz'), it's poisonous!

There are all kinds of stories about him and some people claim that anyone he spits on will always return to the city of Solothurn.

83

Symbols of Switzerland

Helvetia

Helvetia is considered the grand old lady of Switzerland. She is usually portrayed in a long, flowing gown, carrying or holding a spear and a shield that is decorated with the Swiss emblem. This motherly figure was introduced in the 17th century and gained importance when the Helvetic Confederation was established in 1848 and Switzerland became a federal state. The name Helvetia can still be found on coins and stamps and she is depicted on the 50-centime, one-franc, and two-franc coins.

The Latin name 'Confoederatio Helvetica' was introduced so as not to offend any of the four language groups. The word 'Helvetica' derives from the Helvetians, the people who lived in ancient times in what is now Switzerland.

Helvetia on the Middle Bridge in Basel

William Tell

William Tell is a legendary Swiss hero from the village of Bürglen in the canton of Uri. He is said to have fought for the freedom of the local people and liberation from the Habsburg rulers. In 1307 he openly defied the Habsburg bailiff Hermann Gessler, who forced him to shoot an apple off his son's head with his crossbow. Although Tell hit the apple without harming his son, he was arrested for threatening Gessler's life. On the way to the prison cell, he managed to escape and shoot Gessler. Tell's resistance and heroic deed supposedly inspired his countrymen to start an uprising and free themselves from the yoke of the Habsburg oppressors.

William Tell stamps

According to the legend, this incident happened in 1307, only a few years after the Swiss Confederation had been founded in 1291.

William Tell monument in Altdorf

How Switzerland was founded

In 1291 a few men from central Switzerland (the cantons of Uri, Schwyz and Nidwalden) gathered on the Rütli meadow and pledged to form an everlasting alliance. That was the beginning of the Swiss Confederation.

In 1848, after having fought many wars and civil wars, the cantons decided it was time for Switzerland to become a federal state with a constitution.

Flag

The Swiss flag is square unlike all other flags of the world except the one of the Vatican City. Switzerland's flag consists of a white cross on a red background. The arms of the cross are the same length but one sixth longer than they are broad.

The flag dates back to the late Middle Ages when Switzerland still belonged to the German Empire. In 1240 the canton of Schwyz, one of the founding members of the Swiss Confederation supporting the German emperor in wars, was allowed to carry a red flag and one with the cross as a holy sign. Those two flags eventually became the characteristic Swiss flag. The Red Cross chose to base its emblem on the Swiss flag but to reverse the colors.

Anthem

The Swiss Psalm or Swiss National Anthem dates back to the 19th century. In 1841 Leonhard Widmer, songwriter and publisher, wrote a patriotic poem that Alberik Zwyssig set to music. Since the song was very popular, it was officially declared the national anthem on April 1, 1981, and is sung in German, French, Italian and Romansh.

We are ready to fight for self-rule and independence and will always remain loyal to each other.

'Schweizerpsalm'

Trittst im Morgenrot daher,
Seh' ich dich im Strahlenmeer,
Dich, du Hocherhabener, Herrlicher!
Wenn der Alpenfirn sich rötet,
Betet, freie Schweizer betet!
Eure fromme Seele ahnt,
Gott, den Herrn, im hehren Vaterland.

When the morning skies grow red
and over us their radiance shed
Thou, O Lord, appeareth in their light
when the alps glow bright with splendour
for you feel and understand
that he dwelleth in this land.

Wow, we've seen and learned so much about Switzerland. Let's write to Uncle George!

DEAR UNCLE GEORGE

SWITZERLAND IS FUN.
TERE ARE LOTS OF
CASTLES, TRAINS AND
FUNNY PLACES AND
&THINGS TO VISIT AND
YUMMY CHOCOLATE AND NOT
ALL THE CHEESE HAS
GOT HOLES AND PEOPLE
SPEACK FUNNILY.
ANGELA SAYS THEY
SPEAK Þ DIFFERENT
LANGUAGES!

PLEASE COME SOON!

MISS YOU

THOMAS

Subject: greetings from Switzerland
From: swisskids@bergli.ch
To: unclegeorge@bergli.ch

Dear Uncle George,

Remember how sad I was to move away? I'm glad you told me I'd like it here when I get to know some Swiss kids and learn more about Switzerland. Guess what! You are right. We've learned so much from our friend Angela and her books. We have a lot of fun going through them with her and finding tons of great things to do.

I'm so glad you are coming to vist. There are lots of fun places we want to take you to. There's so much to tell you about.

Angela is moving away and I'm very sad about that. She's leaving some of her books with us so that we can show them to you. That way, you will enjoy it more here too. Books are really fun. I want to become a bookseller someday.

I can't wait until you visit. I hope you arrive ON TIME! Remember, that's important here.

Susy

Facts in Brief
Switzerland

Names

Schweiz, Suisse, Svizzera, Svizra.

Official names

'Confoederatio Helvetica': Schweizerische Eidgenossen-
schaft, Confédération suisse, Confederazione Svizzera,
Confederaziun svizra.

When Switzerland became a federal state in 1848, the
Latin name "Confoederatio Helvetica" was introduced.

CH is the abbreviation of Confoederatio Helvetica,
which you see on car number plates.

Helvetica
Helvetica
Helvetica
Helvetica

*Did you know that one of the most widely used type-
faces today is called Helvetica? It was designed by
Edouard Hoffmann and Max Miedinger, two graphic
designers from Münchenstein near Basel.*

Official languages

German, French, Italian, Romansh

Capital

Bern, Berne, Berna, Berna

Area

41,285 km² (approx. 10,201,746 acres or
15,940 square miles)

Flag

White cross on a red background – each arm of
the cross is 1/6th longer than its width.

National motto, flower, animal

There is no Swiss national motto, flower or animal, but
some cantons have a motto or animal. The edelweiss
has the status of an unofficial national flower.

UR	SZ	OW	NW	LU	ZH	GL	ZG	BE	FR	SO	BS	BL
1291	1291	1291	1291	1332	1351	1352	1352	1353	1481	1481	1501	150

Borders	1,882 km (1,170 miles)
Largest extention Dimensions	North - south: 220 km (137 miles) West - east: 348 km (216 miles)
Elevation	Highest: Monte Rosa ('Dufourspitze'), 4,634 meters / 15.203 feet above sea level Lowest: Lake Maggiore ('Lago Maggiore'), 193 meters / 633 feet above sea level
Time zone	Central Europe (GMT +1 hour)
Population	About 7.5 million people
Swiss National Day	August 1
Money	Swiss francs (CHF) conversions: 1 Swiss franc = 100 Rappen (centimes)

100 centimes = 20 x Rappen

100 centimes = 10 x Rappen

100 centimes = 5 x Rappen

100 centimes = 2 x Rappen

SH	AR	AI	SG	GR	AG	TG	TI	VD	VS	NE	GE	JU

501	1513	1513	1803	1803	1803	1803	1803	1803	1815	1815	1815	1979

Canton of Berne

Population	958,000
Capital	Berne
Main industry	Medical technology, hydroelectricity, telecommunications and IT, tourism, vegetable growing in the Seeland area, watch-making industry in the Biel and Bernese Jura areas
A typical animal, plant, place or event	Bears and the Bear Pit
Something children do in their free time	Swim in the Aare river
Traditional festival	'Chästeilet' in Justistal and other valleys in autumn. The cheese produced in the mountains during summer is divided between the owners of the cows. 'Zibelemärit' onion market in Berne in November.
Special attractions	'Aareleuchten', small lights float down the Aare river on August 1

This cow in Justistal is all dressed up for the festivity of coming back home again in autumn from the summer spent grazing on an alp.

Zytglogge (Clock Tower) in Berne

Freilichtmuseum Ballenberg, an open-air museum displaying old houses from all over Switzerland (www.ballenberg.ch)

Forest jump (www.forestjump.ch)

Sensorium at the Rüttihubelbad is a museum where you can watch, touch and experiment. Walk around and try out the 40 fun stations. (www.sensorium.ch).

Take the Märlibahn train HOPP to the top of the Brienzer Rothorn while listening to a lovely story. Then hike the Panorama path. (www.brienz-rothorn-bahn.ch).

Canton of Zurich

Population	1,273,000
Capital	Zurich
Main industry	Agriculture, banking, insurance, paper industry, science, university
A typical animal, plant, place or event	Lion
Something children do in their free time	Swim in Lake Zurich
Traditional festivals	'Sechsilüte' in Zurich in April, especially the children's parade, see page 49. 'Knabenschiessen' in Zurich in September, see page 49. 'Räbeliechtliumzug' in Richterswil in October/November, see page 47.
Special attractions	'Atzmännig' in Goldingen: enjoy the ride down the 700-meter long slide or take a long hike (www.atzmaennig.ch). Zurich Palmen- und Tropenhaus (www.stadt-zuerich.ch/stadtgaertnerei) Zurich Zoo (www.zoo.ch), especially the Masoala Tropical Rain Forest Technorama (The Swiss Science Center) in Winterthur, see page 77 (www.technorama.ch)

Don't forget to visit the Masoala Rain Forest at the Zurich Zoo!

Zurich as seen from the Quai Bridge

Canton of Basel-Stadt

Population	186,000
Capital	Basel
Main industry	Pharmaceutical and chemical industries, financial services, logistics and transport

A typical animal, plant, place or event	'Vogel Gryff' fountains as shown in the picture
Traditional fesival	'Vogel Gryff' festivity, usually in January Basler 'Fasnacht' (carnival), see page 46
Special attractions	Basel Zoo (www.zoobasel.ch) Fauteuil Theater (www.fauteuil.ch) Basler Marionetten Theater (www.baslermarionettentheater.ch). Basel Herbstmesse, autumn fair and fun fair (www.basel.org)

Canton of Basel-Landschaft

Population	266,000
Capital	Liestal
Main industry	Salt production
A typical animal, plant, place or event	Cherry trees
Traditional festival	'Chienbäse' in Liestal, a literally hot festival where wagons and people carry huge burning 'brooms' or piles of wood through the city (www.chienbaese.ch)
Special attraction	Augusta Raurica, extraordinary Roman museum (www.augusta-raurica.ch)

Canton of Solothurn

Population	248,000
Capital	Solothurn
Main industry	Agriculture, manufacturing, microelectronics
A typical animal, plant, place or event	The people of Solothurn have a special relationship with the number eleven. First of all, Solothurn was the 11th canton to join the Confederation. The picturesque Old Town has 11 churches and chapels, 11 historical fountains, and 11 towers. Its St. Ursen Cathedral has 11 altars and 11 bells.
Traditional festival	'Willimann' in Bärschwil, a festival to say goodbye to winter by burning a large doll made of straw.
Special attraction	Dinosaur tracks in the quarry in Lommiswil

Canton of Aargau

Population	569,000
Capital	Aarau
Main industry	Agriculture, basic research, electricity production from hydropower and nuclear power, rich in mineral resources
A typical animal, plant, place or event	Carrots and sugar beets Sauriermuseum Museum in Frick (www.sauriermuseum-frick.ch)
Traditional festival	'Bachfischet', cleaning up the river in Aarau and lantern parade in September. 'Sternensingen' in Wettingen in December. 'Eierleset' in Effingen, a relay race where participants have to pick up as many eggs as possible.

Canton of Schaffhausen

Population	73,700
Capital	Schaffhausen
Main industry	Wine-making, production of machinery and metal goods, watch making and jewellery, hydroelectric power plant generating electricity for export
A typical animal, plant, place or event	Munot, a medieval fortress Rhine Falls in Neuhausen, largest in Europe, see picture on page 17 (www.rhinefalls.ch)
Traditional festival	'Kinderfest' in summer with games and fireworks
Speical attractions	'Herbstfeste' in villages and towns in October (www.schaffhausen-tourismus.ch) 'Märlistadt' Stein am Rhein in December (www.stein-am-rhein.ch)

Canton of Thurgau

Population	234,000
Capital	Frauenfeld
Main industry	Apple and pear growing, production of cider, mechanical engineering
A typical animal, plant, place or event	Apple trees
Traditional festival	'Bochselnacht' in Weinfelden , on Thursday before Christmas with a rutabaga lantern parade 'Lichterschwemmen' in Islikon in spring, children carrying lanterns walk to the Tegelbach river where a boat with many lights floats down the river.

Canton of Appenzell I-Rh.

Population	15,000
Capital	Appenzell
Main industry	Agriculture, cheese making, handicrafts, tourism
A typical animal, plant, place or event	Appenzell mountain dogs, rustic peasant art, 'Alpfahrt', festivities to take cows to and from the alps

Canton of Appenzell O-Rh.

Population	52,000
Capital	Herisau (administrative), Trogen (judicial)
Main industry	Agriculture
A typical animal, plant, place or event	Säntis, the highest mountain in eastern Switzerland
Traditional festivals	'Alpfahrt', festivals to take cows to and from the alps 'Silvesterkläuse', New Year celebrations on January 13 'Viehschau', cattle markets (www.appenzell.ch)

Canton of St. Gallen

Visit Knies Kinderzoo in Rapperswil

Population	458,000
Capital	St. Gallen
Main industry	Agriculture, embroidery, optical technology
A typical animal, plant, place or event	'St. Galler Bratwurst' and 'Schublig' sausages, and 'Bürli' bread
Traditional festival	'Eis-zwei-Geissebei' in Rapperswil in February, sausages are thrown out of the town hall window.
Special attractions	Abbey library in St. Gallen (www.stiftsbibliothek.ch) Olma fair (www.olma-messen.ch)

Canton of Lucerne

Population	356,000
Capital	Lucerne
Main industry	Tourism, dairy food production, glas blowing in Sarnen and Hergiswil, agriculture with crops, fruit, cattle
A typical animal, plant, place or event	'Kappelenbrücke', a beautiful covered bridge with historical artworks
Traditional festival	Luzerner 'Fasnacht', carnival, see page 46 'Lichterschwemmen' in Emmensee in March where kids let their wooden constructions float down the river.
Special attractions	Swiss Museum of Transport and Communication (www.verkehrshaus.ch) Glacier Garden with a mirror labyrinth (www.gletschergarten.ch) Schongi-Land park with a toboggan run, games and trails (www.schongiland.ch) Gold panning in Fontannenbach near Willisau (www.goldwasch-tour.ch)

Canton of Zug

Population	106,000
Capital	Zug
Main industry	Electronics industry, finance, pharmaceuticals and high-tech sectors
A typical animal, plant, place or event	Zytturm, a 52-meter high tower with a dungeon over-looking the city, the Pulverturm, and the Huwilerturm
Traditional festival	'Märlisunntig', fairytales on the second Sunday during advent (www.zuger-maerlisunntig.ch)
Special attraction	Höllgrotten in Baar, the cave pictured on page 15 (www.hoellgrotten.ch)

Canton of Schwyz

Population	138,000
Capital	Schwyz
A typical animal, plant, place or event	'Chinesenfasnacht', a carnival with a Chinese theme held in the city of Schwyz
Traditional festival	'Klausjagen' on December 5 in Küssnacht am Rigi where groups with beautifully crafted lanterns on their heads lead a procession of 'Trychler', see picture on page 48.
Special attractions	'Bundesbriefmuseum' with documents about the foundation of Switzerland (www.bundesbriefmuseum.ch) 'Schaukäserei' Schwyzerland, a dairy (www.milchstrasse.ch)

Canton of Uri

Population	35,000
Capital	Altdorf
Main industry	Agriculture, electrical industry, mechanical engineering, tourism
A typical animal, plant, place or event	William Tell statue and theater performances in Altdorf
Traditional festival	Carnival with the characher 'Drapoling aus Amsteg'
Special attractions	Tasting many different kinds of cheese 'Sagen'-Trails about the myths, tales and legends of the region (www.top-of-uri.ch)

Traffic jam on the Klausenpass

97

Canton of Obwalden

Population	33,000
Capital	Sarnen
Main industry	Agriculture with livestock and dairy farming, tourism
A typical animal, plant, place or event	Schützenhaus von Landenberg in Sarnen 'Moorlandschaft', the moorlands around Glaubenberg
Traditional festival	'Älplerchilbi', the harvest festival in October

Canton of Nidwalden

Population	40,000
Capital	Stans
Main industry	Agriculture, mechanical engineering
A typical animal, plant, place or event	Cable cars and funiculars to Klewenalp and Stanser-horn, the Winkelried statue and fountain in Stans
Traditional festival	'Älplerchilbi', the harvest festival in October
Special attraction	'Wirzweli', fun park near Dallenwil (www.wirzweli.ch)

Canton of Glarus

Population	38,000
Capital	Glarus
Main industry	Agriculture, mechanical engineering, tourism
A typical animal, plant, place or event	The sun shines through the 'Martinsloch' hole of a mountain on the church in Elm twice a year.
Traditional festival	Festival of floating lights in Bilten in March
Special attractions	Braunwald 'Zwerg Bartli' (www.braunwald.ch)

Canton of Geneva

Population	431,000
Capital	Geneva
Main endeavors	Headquarters of the World Trade Organisation (WTO), UN High Commission for Human Rights (UNHCHR), International Committee of the Red Cross, humanitarian organizations for peace and disarmament, economical development, for the environment, and many more.
A typical animal, plant, place or event	Fountain in the lake, boat excursions on Lac Léman 'Escalade' festival (see page 47)

Canton of Fribourg

Population	254,000
Capital	Fribourg
Main industry	Agriculture, food industry, especially cheese, chocolate
A typical animal, product, place or event	Cows – especially the black and white ones, Vacherin cheese and fondue
Traditional festival	'Bénichon', a fun fair celebrating the return from the alps, with culinary delights like mutton with mashed potatoes, meringue for dessert, music and dance
Special attractions	Fribourg has 6 tours through town, some on scooters and a mini-train (www.fribourgtourism.ch)
	Gruyères, a beautiful medieval town
	'Papiliorama' in Kerzers has hundreds of butterflies and humming birds (www.papiliorama.ch)

This street in bilingual Fribourg is called 'short way' but in German it seems much shorter than in French.

Canton of Neuchâtel

Population	169,000
Capital	Neuchâtel
Main industry	Watch and high-tech industries, grape-growing and wine-making

Special attractions — Fêtes de Vendanges, the biggest wine-growers' festival in Switzerland

Asphalt mines in Val de Travers (www.gout-region.ch)

Laténium in Hauterive, a park and archeological museum (www.latenium.ch)

Summer sledding at Féeline, Val de Travers (www.feeline.ch)

Underground mill in Le Locle, Col-des-Roches (www.lesmoulins.ch)

Canton of Jura

Population	70,000
Capital	Delémont
Main industry	Agriculture, livestock breeding, mechanical engineering, watch-making industries

A typical animal, plant, place or event — Horses grazing, nature and landscape
'Marché-Concours', festival of horses in August in Saignelégier (www.marcheconcours.ch)

Special attractions — Les Prés d'Orvin: Forest Jump where you can play Tarzan (www.bisonranch.ch)

Juraparc near Vallorbe has bison, bears and wolves living there (www.juraparc.ch)

Canton of Vaud

Population	654,000
Capital	Lausanne
Main industry	Grape-growing and wine-making, high-tech industries
A typical animal, plant, place or event	Grapes and vineyards
Traditional festival	'Fêtes du Bois' in Lausanne, a parade of kids wearing colorful costumes at the end of June 'Brandons' in Payerne and Moudon to welcome spring by burning 'bohomme hiver'
Special attractions	'Planète Jeux' in La Croix, Lutry, a park with all kinds of games (www.planete-jeux.ch)
	Salt mines in Bex (www.mines.ch)
	World Tracasset Championships in Epesses – grape-growers on their three-wheeled vehicles take part in a race (www.topio.ch/tracasset)

Canton of Valais

Population	292,000
Capital	Sion
Main industry	Tourism, fruit and grape-growing, wine-making
A typical animal, plant, place or event	Cow-fighting competitions on Sundays from spring to autumn where the strongest cow wins a beautiful bell
Traditional festival	'Tschäggättä' with masked figures like in this picture in the Lötschental
Special attractions	Go see real dinosaur tracks, Emosson (www.emosson-lac.ch)
	Adventure forest in Vercoin (www.matterhornstate.com)

Watch out for such 'Tschäggättä' figures in Lötschental!

Canton of Grisons

Population	188,000
Capital	Chur
Main industry	Tourism, agriculture
A typical animal, plant, place or event	Ibex
Traditional festival	'Schlitteda', a procession of horse-drawn sleighs in January 'Chalandamarz' in Zuoz to welcome spring with bells
Special attractions	Cavaglia, the giants' cauldrons, or glacial moulin potholes of Cavaglia formed during the last ice age (www.valposchiavo.ch)

In Disentis and Sedrun you can build your own iglu and spend the night in it or go on snowshoe excursions (www.iglutour.ch)

Percorso Avventura Trail, Maloja in the Engadine, up and down hills and gorges with your harness and hooks, over rope ladders and hanging bridges (www.maloja.ch)

Pradaschier-Churwalden tobogan slide and rope park (www.pradaschier.ch)

Preda-Bergün down-hill scooter trip (www.berguen.ch)

Boys singing at 'Chalandamarz'

Canton of Ticino

Population	323,000
Capital	Bellinzona
Main industry	Tourism, construction and trade industry, agriculture
A typical animal, plant, place or event	Chestnuts, salami
Traditional festival	Chestnut fairs Risottata di Carnevale in Lugano
Special attractions	Swissminiatur in Melide, a park with Switzerland in miniature size to walk aroud and see its main attractions, see picture page 77 (www.swissminiatur.ch)

Good swimmers can discover some sublime swimming holes with crystal-clear mountain water in the Verzasca and Maggia rivers near Locarno.

Sunshine and beautiful views make Swiss kids want to flock to the canton of Ticino any time of the year.

10 km   0   10   20   30

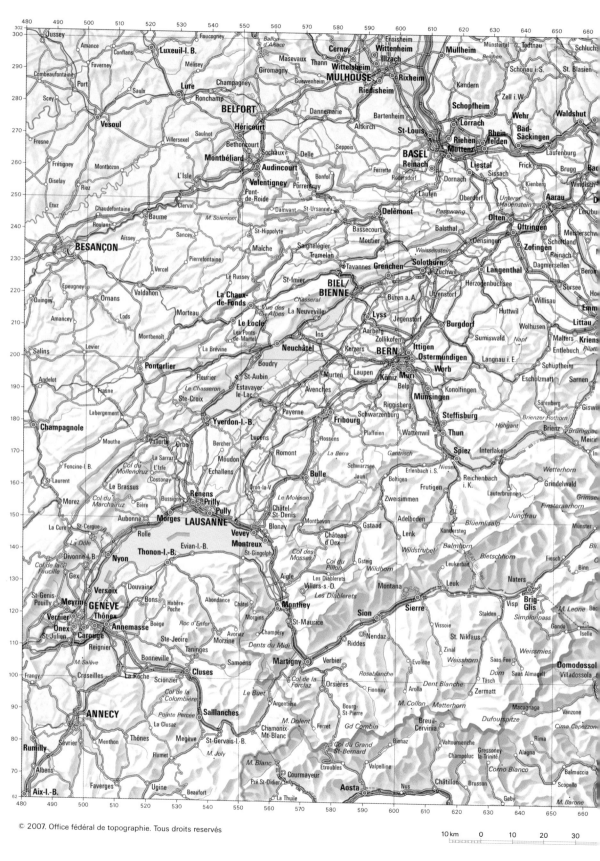

10 km   0   10   20   30

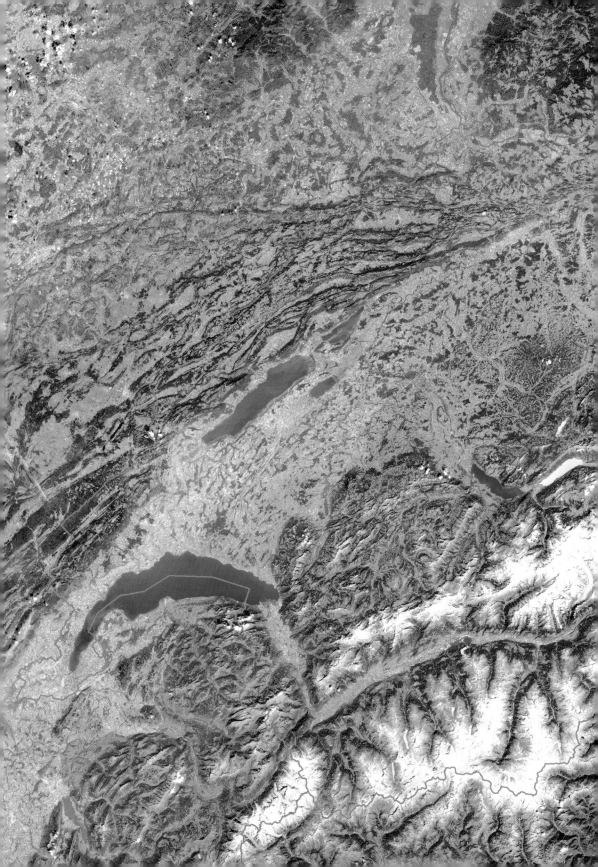

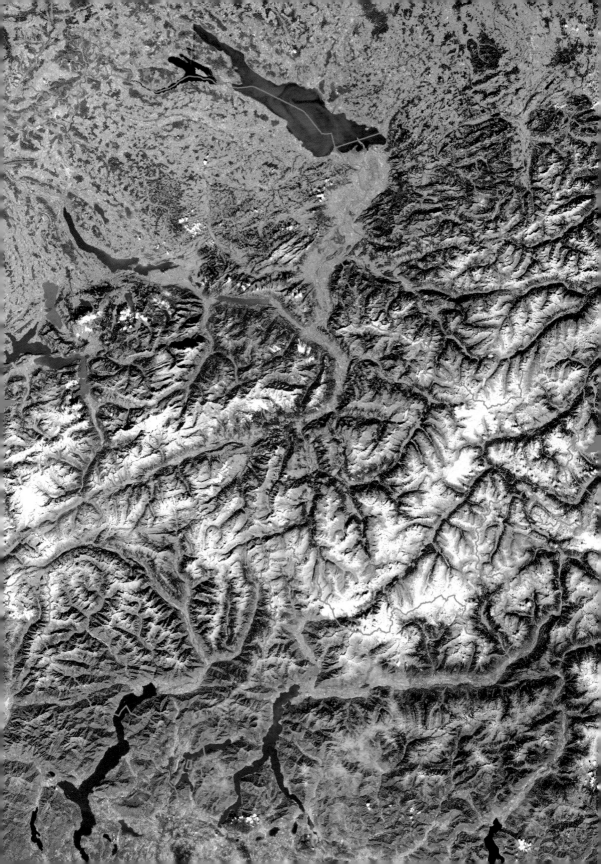

Places to visit with children

Castles

Information and pictures of over 800 castles in
Switzerland (www.swisscastles.ch)

'Castles in Switzerland' lists the castles according to
cantons and offers information about them and
links to the websites (www.burgen.ch)

Let's go!

AG	Lenzburg, Lenzburg Castle (www.ag.ch/lenzburg)
	Seengen, Hallwyl Castle, Seengen (www.schlosshallwyl.ch)
BE	Burgdorf Castle, Museum documenting the history of the search
	for gold in Switzerland, and Museum für Völkerkunde
	(www.schloss-burgdorf.ch)
GR	Ehrenfels Castle in Sils is a Youth Hostel (www.youthhostel.ch)
LU	Gelfingen, Heidegg Castle (www.heidegg.ch)
NW	Stans, Winkelried Castle (Winkelriedhaus)
SH	Stein am Rhein, Hohenklingen Castle (www.hohenklingen.ch)
VD	Montreux, Chillon Castle (www.chillon.ch)
	La Sarraz Castle – furnished castle and horse museum
	(www.muche.ch)
	Morges Castle and Museums – artillery, tin figure and
	historical museum (www.chateau-morges.ch)
VS	Brig, Stockalper's Castle
ZH	Kyburg, Kyburg Castle (www.schlosskyburg.ch)

Caves
www.grotte.ch

Cheese dairies

AR	Stein, Apppenzeller Schaukäserei, (www.schaukaeserei.ch)
BE	Affoltern i.E., Emmentaler Schaukäserei AG (ESK) (www.showdairy.ch)
FR	Pringy/Gruyères, La Maison du Gruyère (www.lamaisondugruyere.ch)
	Moléson-sur-Gruyères, Mountain Cheese Dairy (www.fromagerie-alpage.ch)

Chocolate factories

AG	Buchs, Chocolat Frey AG (www.chocolatfrey.ch)
FR	Broc, Cailler Chocolate Factory (www.cailler.ch)
ZH	Kilchberg, Lindt & Sprüngli

Lama trekking in various places in Switzerland

BE   Wyssachen (www.lama-ranch.ch); Wilderswil (www.lamatrek-jungfrauregion.ch)

Museums

AG   Aarau, Naturama: three floors with themes of past, present, future (www.naturama.ch)
     Frick, Sauriermuseum: a skeleton of a plateosaurus and many fossils on exhibit
          (www.sauriermuseum-frick.ch)
     Baden, Kindermuseum (www.kindermuseum.ch)
BE   Berne, Museum of Communication: interactive tour of various forms of communication
          (www.mfk.ch)
     Berne, Kindermuseum Creaviva at the Zentrum Paul Klee (www.zpk.org)
     Berne, Natural History Museum (www.nmbe.ch)
     Brienz, Swiss Open-Air Museum Ballenberg (www.ballenberg.ch)
     Rüttihubelbad, Sensorium: 40 fun stations (www.sensorium.ch)
BS   Basel, Cartoon Museum (www.cartoonmuseum.ch)
     Basel, Historisches Museum Basel is in four locations: the Historischen Museum in the
          Barfüsserkirche, the Haus zum Kirschgarten, the Musikmuseum, and the Kutschen-
          museum (www.hmb.ch)
     Basel, Puppenhausmuseum (doll house museum) (www.puppenhausmuseum.ch)
     Riehen, Spielzeugmuseum (toy museum) (www.riehen.ch)
BL   Seewen, Museum für Musikautomaten (music box museum) (www.musee-suisse.ch/seewen)
GE   Geneva, Natural History Museum (www.ville-ge.ch/musinfo)
     Geneva, Red Cross & Red Crescent Museum (www.micr.ch)
GR   Chur, Bündner Naturmuseum (www.naturmuseum.gr.ch)
     Poschiavo, Art Museum Casa Console (www.valposchiavo.ch)
     Poschiavo, Weaver's Workshop (www.valposchiavo.ch)
JU   Vallorbe, Railway museum (www.vallorbe.ch)
LU   Swiss Museum of Traffic and Communication (www.verkehrshaus.ch)
NE   La Chaux-de-Fonds, International Clock and Watch museum (www.mih.ch)
     Neuchâtel, Natural History Museum (www.museum-neuchatel.ch)
SH   Stein am Rhein, Museum Lindwurm (www.museum-lindwurm.ch)
SO   Solothurn, Natural History Museum (www.naturmuseum-so.ch)
     Balstal, Alt Falkenstein Klus (www.museum-alt-falkenstein.ch)
TG   Kreuzlingen, Seemuseum (www.seemuseum.ch)
     Frauenfeld, Naturmuseum und Museum für Archäologie Thurgau (www.museen.tg.ch)
VD   Vevey, Alimentarium (the Food Museum) (www.alimentarium.ch)
     Blonay-Chamby, Railway Museum: rides on a narrow-gauge line (www.blonay-chamby.ch)
     Lausanne, Olympics Museum (www. museum.olympic.org)
     Lucens, Sherlock-Holmes-Museum (www.lucens.ch)

Places to visit with children

ZH   Aathal, Dinosauriermuseum with lots of fossils (www.sauriermuseum.ch)
       Bubikon, Ritterhaus (www.ritterhaus.ch)
       Dübendorf, Flieger Flab Museum (www.airforcecenter.ch)
       Winterthur, Technorama, the Swiss Science Center (www.technorama.ch)
       Zurich, Nordamerika Native Museum: information about Native Americans and other
           indegenous people. (www.nonam.ch)
       Zurich, Kulturama: Museum des Menschen (www.kulturama.ch)

Nature

Birdwatching around Switzerland (www.birdlife.ch)

Pools

SG   Bad Ragaz, thermal spa (www.spavillage.ch)
SZ   Pfäffikon, Alpamare: indoor and outdoor pools, artificial waves (www.alpamare.ch)
VD   Yverdon-les-Bains, thermal pools (www.cty.ch)
       La Plage de Buchillon (near Morges) is an excellent beach for families
VS   Leukerbad, Burgerbad thermal baths (www.burgerbad.ch)
       Le Bouveret on the shores of Lac Léman: a water adventure world (www.aquaparc.ch)
       and the Swiss Vapeur Parc (www.swissvapeur.ch)

Trails

AI   Kronberg, bobsled run and park with ropes for climbing (www.kronberg.ch)
BE   Grimmialp-Diemtigtal, Grimmimutz has an abundance of activities for children
          (www.diemtigtal.ch).
       Lenk, Murmeli Trail (marmot or groundhog trail, also a lynx adventure trail)
          (www.lenk.ch)
       Mürren, from Allmendhubel, Children's Adventure Trail (www.schilthorn.ch)
       Meiringen, Mägisalp im Haslital, 5 km long Muggestutz dwarf path with caves and ladders
          (www.meiringen-hasliberg.ch)
FR   Moléson-sur-Gruyères, summer sledding, climbing (www.moleson.ch)
       Charmey, Charme(y) Aventures: five skywalking adventure paths in the trees
          (www.charmeyaventure.ch)
GL   Filzbach, Habergschwänd, on the Kerenzerberg, a 1.3 km long toboggan run
          (www.kerenzerberg.ch).
GR   Lenzerheide, Globiweg hiking trail (www.lenzerheide.ch)
SG   Flawil, 'Fun City Kartbahn', a carting rink (www.kartbahnflawil.ch)
       Bad Ragaz, Heidi and Peter excursions and trails (www.spavillage.ch)

SO Balmberg, Seilpark (rope park) offers rope-climbing trails (www.seilpark-balmberg.ch)

VD Chateau-d'Oex, La Braye mountain top nature trail about ants and a treasure hunt made by the world adventurer Mike Horn (www.telechateaudoex.ch).

VS Col de la Forclaz, an easy hike to the Trient glacier (www.noth.ch/h0116_d.html)

Evionnaz, Labyrinthe adventure (www.labyrinthe.ch). See picture page 113.

Saillon, take Postauto to Montagnon over Hameau des Places, the trail has a spectacular hanging bridge. From Sommet des vignes go back to Saillon (thermal baths www.bainsdesaillon.ch)

Saas Almagell, an adventure trail around the Almagellerhorn crossing hanging bridges (www.saas-almagell.ch)

Saas-Fee, explore the Adventure Forest with different routes of various degrees of difficulty (www.saas-fee.ch) (see summer activities)

Gelmersee, Triftbahn/Triftschlucht, hike across the highest and longest hanging bridge in Europe – 110 m long and 70 m high (www.grimselhotels.ch). See picture page 76.

Zoos

BE Berne, Tierpark Dählhölzli – animal park where kids can feed and pet animals (ww.tierpark-bern.ch)

BS Basel, Zoo Basel, visit the Vivarium, the monkey's house and Etoscha house (www.zoobasel.ch)

SG Rapperswil, Circus Knie's children's zoo where kids can feed animals, ride a pony, an elephant or a camel, or watch sea lions demonstrate their amazing skills (www.knieskinderzoo.ch)

SZ Goldau, Tierpark (animal park) (www.tierpark.ch)

VD Servion, Tropiquarium with a zoo and botanical park in a tropical climate all year round, birds and reptiles in tropical greenhouses, parks, and aviaries (www.tropiquarium.ch)

ZH Zurich Zoo (www.zoo.ch)

Get lost in the biggest labyrinth in the world at the 'Labyrinthe Adventure' in Evionnaz, canton Valais.

Useful links

Switzerland tourism
Information about interesting and popular tourist destinations in Switzerland (www.myswitzerland.ch, click on family)

Information about activities for children
KIDS.CH   www.kids.ch
kids.en-force   www.kids.en-force.ch

Index of topics

Index of topics

Acknowledgements

Many people came to our rescue in providing their generous assistance, contributions, ideas and feedback to make this book possible:

Robin Bognuda
Nico and Susanne Fichinni Borgeaud
Anne-Louise Bornstein
Cantonal Tourist Offices
Gregorio Caruso
Hilary Cole
Patricia Eckert
Kris Germann
Bernhard Gloor
Isabel Gut
Peter Habicht
Katie Hayoz
Mary Hogan
Robin Hull
Viviane Kammermann
Walter Loeliger
Alan Lyons
Scott MacRae
Andrew Rushton
Fabienne Schaller
Jeanne Schaller
Andrew Shields
Monique and Tom Spencer
Loretta Strauch
Sue Style
Tabea Utz

Bank Morgan Stanley AG

Swiss Air-Rescue Rega, which is popularly known in Switzerland by kids of all ages as the 'Rega', brings medical assistance and physicians to the scene of emergencies, and assists mountain farmers to rescue injured livestock (www.rega.ch).

See the following websites for more information about Switzerland:

www.swissinfo.org
www.swissworld.ch
about education: www.educa.ch
for statistics: www.statistik.admin.ch
about the Swiss Federal Railways: www.sbb.ch
about tourism: www.myswitzerland.com
about politics: www.swisspolitics.org
about environmental issues: www.umwelt-schweiz.ch

Photo credits, sources and permissions

Page	Topic	Photo credits and copyright notices
13	Diavolezza with Mount Palü	Emanuel Ammon / AURA
13	Rolling hills in Menzingen, Zug	Andreas Busslinger / AURA
13	Aare River near Solothurn from Mount Weissenstein	Andreas Busslinger / AURA
13	Juf in Averstal GR	Emanuel Ammon / AURA
13	View of Mount Pilatus from the Rigi Kulm	Stefano Schröter / AURA
13	Morteratsch Glacier	Andreas Busslinger / AURA
13	'Findling' rocks near Flüelen	Emanuel Ammon / AURA
14	Eiger, Mönch, and Jungfrau mountains	Urs Möckli / AURA
15	Aletsch Glacier	Urs Möckli / AURA
15	Sheep traffic jam in the Aletsch region	Hulda Jossen / AURA
15	'Höllgrotten' caves, Baar	Emanuel Ammon / AURA
17	Paddle steamer on Lac Léman	Emanuel Ammon / AURA
17	Apartment buildings on the Lake of Lugano	Emanuel Ammon / AURA
17	View of Bürgenstock from Mount Rigi	Emanuel Ammon / AURA
17	Rhine Falls	Emanuel Ammon / AURA
17	Castle of Chillon, Montreux	Emanuel Ammon / AURA
18	Spring in the hills made from moraines	Andreas Busslinger / AURA
18	Photo of cloud	MeteoSchweiz/Kaeslin
18	Lightning	Stefano Schröter / AURA
18	'Wasserhose' water spout cloud	Hans-Peter Milt
19	Autumn leaves	Loretta Strauch
19	Damages from hurricane Lothar in Nidwalden	Emnuel Ammon / AURA
19	Sea of fog	Henrik Norborg
19	Winter path	Loretta Strauch
20	Photographs of clouds	MeteoSchweiz/Kaeslin
20	Red sky over the sea of fog at Mount Rigi	Dianne Dicks
26-27	Photos of trees	Fotos von Jean-Denis Godet/Arboris Verlag
30	Rösti on plate	Photograph with permission of Laurent Flutsch Musée romain de Lausanne-Vidy
36	Swatch watches	Swatch Ltd., 2007
37	Snail at goal	Jenö Gösi / AURA
38	Rigi Song 'Vo Luzern uf Weggis zue'	Music and lyrics in 1832 by Johann Lüthi (public domain)
39	Swiss steak	Source unknown
39	Swiss roll	Dianne Dicks
39	Battle of Näfels (1388)	From Diebold Schilling's Luzerner Bilderchronik 1513
40	Alphorn player	Albrecht von Haller's *The Alps*, copyright 1987 Walter Amstutz De Clivo Press, Dübendorf
41	Cog railway to Stoos	Emanuel Ammon / AURA
41	Immigrants to the United States	Frank Leslie's illustrated newspaper, 1887 July 2, pp 324-325, public domain
42	Coins	Eidgenössische Münzstätte Swissmint, Bern
42	Shopping trolley	Emanuel Ammon / AURA
46	Fasnacht Basel	Kurt Wyss, Basel
46	Fasnacht Lucerne	Emanuel Ammon / AURA
47	'Räbeliechtli' (rutabaga lanterns)	Michael Sengers, Zurich
47	Escalade in Geneva	Emanuel Ammon / AURA
47	*Räbeliechtli* song	Music and lyrics by Johann Lüthi in 1832 (public domain)
48	Large bells from Appenzell	Loretta Strauch
48	Boys with bells	Emanuel Ammon / AURA
48	Klausjagen in Küssnacht am Rigi	Emanuel Ammon / AURA
49	Sechseläuten in Zurich	Emanuel Ammon / AURA
50	Christmas tree	Emanuel Ammon / AURA

Photo credits

50	'Grittibänz' (Santa bread)	Emanuel Ammon / AURA
50	Santa in the bookshop	Dianne Dicks
51	Santa on skis	Emanuel Ammon / AURA
51	'Schlitteda' (sleighs and horses) at Silvaplana	Emanuel Ammon / AURA
52	Bunny bread	Emanuel Ammon / AURA
52	Easter egg	Emanuel Ammon / AURA
52	Easter chocolate bunny	Emanuel Ammon / AURA
52	Children's playground at Fronalpstock	Emanuel Ammon / AURA
53	'Fahnenschwinger' (flag-thrower)	Emanuel Ammon / AURA
53	'Rütlischwur' engraving about 1860	Peter Ammon / AURA
53	Children with August 1 lanterns	Emanuel Ammon / AURA
56	Inline skating	Jenö Gösi / AURA
56	Badminton	Emanuel Ammon / AURA
56	Sliding	Emanuel Ammon / AURA
56	Swimming at Lake Lauerz	Emanuel Ammon / AURA
57	'Cervelat' on an open fire	Andreas Busslinger / AURA
57	Climbing	Emanuel Ammon / AURA
57	Picnic in the forest	Emanuel Ammon / AURA
57	Street hockey	Emanuel Ammon / AURA
57	Sleeping child	Andreas Busslinger / AURA
57	Young Swiss wrestlers	Eidgenössischer Schwingerverband
58	House in Appenzell	Loretta Strauch
58	Goat living on a balcony in Guarda, canton Grisons	Loretta Strauch
58	Apartments with balconies	Emanuel Ammon / AURA
59	Houses in Oberstammheim-Hüttwilersee	Emanuel Ammon / AURA
59	Residential area in Reinach, Basel-Landschaft	Emanuel Ammon / AURA
59	Residential area in Adligenswil	Emanuel Ammon / AURA
60	Bread	Emanuel Ammon / AURA
60	Birchermüesli	Emanuel Ammon / AURA
60	Cheese plate	Emanuel Ammon / AURA
60	'Bündnerteller'	Emanuel Ammon / AURA
60	'Bernerplatte'	Emanuel Ammon / AURA
60	Salad plate	Emanuel Ammon / AURA
60	'Risotto'	Marcel Grubenmann / AURA
60	'Pizokel'	Marcel Grubenmann / AURA
60	'Raclette'	Emanuel Ammon / AURA
61	Carrot cake	Emanuel Ammon / AURA
61	Crème caramel	Emanuel Ammon / AURA
61	Strawberry tart	Emanuel Ammon / AURA
61	'Birnenbrot' of Engelberg	Loretta Strauch
61	Edelweiss chocolate	Emanuel Ammon / AURA
61	'Vermicelles'	Emanuel Ammon / AURA
61	Plum pie	Loretta Strauch
63	Red and green pedestrian lights	Dianne Dicks
63	Vests for kids going to kindergarten	Dianne Dicks
64	Franz Hohler reading	with permission of Franz Hohler
64	Book lover with Globi	Andreas Busslinger / AURA
64	*Tschipo* by Franz Hohler	Cover by Thomas M. Müller:
		2006 Deutscher Taschenbuch Verlag, Munich
64	*Asterix in Switzerland*	*Astérix chez les Helvètes* © 1970 Goscinny / Uderzo
65	*Heidi* by Johanna Spyri	Published by Children Classics, an imprint of
		Random House Value Publishing, New York
65	*A Bell for Ursli* by Carigiet/Chönz	*Schellen-Ursli* © 1971 Orell Füssli Verlag AG, Zürich
65	*Marta au pays des montgolfières*	G. Zullo, Albertine © Editions La Joie de lire SA, 2001
65	*The Rainbow Fish*	Marcus Pfister © 1992 NordSüd Verlag AG Zurich

* All effort has been made to give credit to the original copyright holders. Contact Bergli Books if you have any questions.

About the authors, illustrator and photographer

Co-author Dianne Dicks

grew up in the States and came to Switzerland a very long time ago intending to stay for just a few weeks on a program of the Experiment in International Living. Now, decades later, she is still 'experimenting', mostly in Basel. She founded Bergli Books in 1990 to publish intercultural books in English that focus on Switzerland. Many books later, she still enjoys the game of trying to understand what makes living here so special. In 2002 she and Angela Joos opened the Bergli Bookshop in Basel, specializing in books and events in English. You might find her happily hiking or cycling somewhere in Switzerland or jogging along the Rhine. Please smile and wave as she goes by! Stop her if you can. Her favorite spot in Switzerland (for swimming and for dreaming) is the elephant rock between Weggis and Vitznau.

Co-autor Katalin Fekete

grew up in Switzerland. Her name is Hungarian but like many kids whose parents came here from someplace else, she is as Swiss as they come. She was fascinated by languages at an early age. After studying English in Switzerland and abroad, she worked in the States in publishing and in Switzerland as a journalist before joining the team at Bergli Books. She particularly enjoys doing research on the Swiss and their ways. When she is not writing or editing (or studying the intricacies of computer software), you'll find her reading books, hiking or playing football with her husband and two sons. Do say 'Grüezi Katalin' (not Katherine) and smile when you see her reading a book on the train between Baden and Basel. Her favorite spot in Switzerland is Lenzerheide/Valbella in winter. Don't forget your skis!

Illustrator Marc Locatelli

was probably born on a bicycle in Zurich. His name may be Italian but to his regret nobody has spoken it in his family for ages. He has cycled in lots of interesting spots in the world. If you see him cycling over his favorite mountain pass, the Susten, say 'Hop hop Marc!' He is a graphic designer and illustrator, especially for educational publications. You might think he is rather shy and quiet until you see him acting silly on stage with his theater group as the long, lanky clown who seems to have outgrown his clothes. His favorite toys are (surprise, surprise) watercolors and a brush. His favorite spot in Switzerland is Greina in the Engadine . He enjoyed most drawing all the bicycles in this book. Guess how many there are! Can you find them? See the solution on page 126.

Photographer Emanuel Ammon

grew up in Lucerne with cameras as his favorite toys. You might find him and his cameras anywhere in the world on assignments as a photojournalist. He and his AURA photo agency are located in the picturesque city of Lucerne. You can explore his archives of outstanding photography at www.emanuel-ammon.ch. Warning: you won't be able to stop looking! Don't say 'cheese' if he aims his camera at you, just be yourself. His favorite photograph in this book is of the water slide in Reiden on page 56.

About Bergli Books

Bergli Books publishes, promotes and distributes books mostly in English that focus on living in Switzerland.

Ticking Along with the Swiss
edited by Dianne Dicks, entertaining and informative personal experiences of many 'foreigners' living in Switzerland.
ISBN 978-3-9520002-4-3.

Ticking Along Too
edited by Dianne Dicks, has more personal experiences, a mix of social commentary, warm admiration and observations of the Swiss as friends, neighbors and business partners.
ISBN 978-3-9520002-1-2.

Ticking Along Free
edited by Dianne Dicks, with more stories about living with the Swiss, this time with also some prominent Swiss writers.
ISBN 978-3-905252-02-6.

Cupid's Wild Arrows –
intercultural romance and its consequences
edited by Dianne Dicks, contains personal experiences of 55 authors living with two worlds in one partnership. ISBN 978-3-9520002-2-9.

Laughing Along with the Swiss
by Paul Bilton has everything you need to know to endear you to the Swiss forever.
ISBN 978-3-905252-01-9.

Once Upon an Alp
by Eugene Epstein. A selection of the best stories from this well-known American/Swiss humorist. ISBN 978-3-905252-05-7.

Swiss Me
by Roger Bonner, illustrations by Edi Barth. A collection of playful stories about living with the Swiss by a Swiss/American humorist.
ISBN 978-3-905252-11-8.

A Taste of Switzerland
by Sue Style, with over 50 recipes that show the richness of this country's diverse gastronomic cultures. ISBN 978-3-9520002-7-4.

Berne –
a portrait of Switzerland's federal capital, of its people, culture and spirit
by Peter Studer (photographs), Walter Däpp, Bernhard Giger and Peter Krebs.
ISBN 978-3-9520002-9-8.

Beyond Chocolate –
understanding Swiss culture
by Margaret Oertig-Davidson, an in-depth discussion of the cultural attitudes and values of the Swiss for newcomers and long-term residents. English edition ISBN 978-3-905252-06-4. German edition ISBN 978-3-905252-10-1.

Hoi – your Swiss German survival guide
by Sergio J. Lievano and Nicole Egger, chock-full of cartoons, tips and encouragement to help you learn Swiss German, includes English and Swiss German dictionaries. English edition ISBN 978-3-905252-13-2. German edition includes German and Swiss German dictionaries ISBN 978-3-905252-14-9.

Lifting the Mask – your guide to Basel Fasnacht
by Peter Habicht, illustrations by Fredy Prack. Whether you are a first-time visitor or a life-long enthusiast, here's all you need to know (and more) to enjoy Basel's famous carnival. English edition ISBN 978-3-905252-04-0. German edition ISBN 978-3-905252-09-5.

Culture Smart Switzerland –
a quick guide to customs and etiquette
by Kendall Maycock provides crucial insights to business culture to help newcomers navigate their way quickly through Swiss life and society.
ISBN 978-3-905252-12-5.

Could you say that again?

Wie bitte, was hast du gesagt?

Was häsch gseit?

It's a great game

Ist doch ein tolles

Isch doch es super

Language card game
You must be joking!

A fun game for ages 7 to 99

Cut out carefully the 32 cards on the pages at the center of this book. Each card has a question or an answer in English, German, Swiss dialect, French, Italian and Romansh.

The 14 blue Question cards are marked with

The 14 white Answer cards and 2 Joker cards are marked with

Instructions for 2 – 4 players:
The game can be played in any of the six languages on the cards.
1. Agree on which language you want to play this game in.
2. Sort the cards with that language face down.
3. Sort again putting the blue Question cards in one deck, the white Answer cards and Jokers in another.
4. Put the deck of blue Question cards with the chosen language face down in the center of the table.
5. Deal out all the white Answer cards to

players who put them with the chosen language face down in a stack in front of them. Depending on the number of players, not all players may have the same number of cards. This does not matter.

The object of the game is to give suitable answers to the questions and get rid of all your Answer cards. Joker cards with YOU MUST BE JOKING! can be used to answer any question. Demonstrate your acting skills, vary the tone of your voice and facial expressions to give a variety of interpretations to your questions and answers. The first player to get rid of all Answer cards is the winner.

Procedure:

Player 1 draws a Question card from the top of the deck on the table, reads it out and puts it at the bottom of the Question card deck.

Player 2 draws the top Answer card in his or her deck and reads it out. If the answer is suitable, then Player 2 can discard that Answer to form a deck next to the Question cards. If it is not suitable, the Answer card has to be kept and the game goes to the next player.
Then Player 2 draws a Question card from the top of the deck, reads it out and the

wahr?

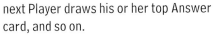

next Player draws his or her top Answer card, and so on.

When it is not clear if the answer is suitable or not, the player wanting to use that card must justify the answer by inventing and explaining a situation where that answer would be appropriate. The other players have to agree that it is a suitable answer, otherwise the player has to keep that Answer card until it can be used in another round.

Three variations of the game:

1. One step further:

Player 1 asks a question, Player 2 answers, then Player 1 has to come up with an invented comment that continues the conversation in a natural way. The two players keep going until someone cannot come up with a further comment. The last player to have made a suitable comment gets an extra benefit by being allowed to lay down one extra Answer card.

2. Playing the game alone:

Put the Question cards and Answer cards face down on the table. Draw from the top of each stack a question and answer. If they suit each other, they can be discarded on separate stacks and you can draw the next Question and Answer cards. If an answer is not suitable, discard it face down next to the first stack of Answer cards. Keep drawing answers and questions until you no longer have any Answer cards.

3. Playing in a new language:

Once you have played this simple game a few times, you will know the questions and answers well. Then you can enjoy playing it in a new language.

Agree with the other players in which language you want to play this game. In this case players can lay out the Answer cards face up in front of them to select what they guess is the most suitable answer. For example, if you agree to play it in Italian and nobody knows how to speak Italian, then just try to read out your question or answer as best you can.

You will know what you are saying because of the text given in other languages on your card. Try to convince the other players by your confident voice that you have the right answer. If they don't believe you, compare the texts of the Question and Answer cards in a language you understand.

The object is, like in real life, to listen carefully to what people say to you in another language and try to guess what the meaning is and give an appropriate answer. Be sure to consider how something is said, not only what is said!

Buon divertimento!
Bien du plaisir!
Viel Spass!
Bun divertiment!

125

Picture contest instructions

Now you know that there is nothing that is 'typical' of Switzerland. Whatever you say about it, it won't apply for the whole country and somebody living here will tell you "maybe that's the way it is where you live but here it is different!" You can enjoy being different too. Like in all countries, it's very difficult to generalize about people, what they think and how they behave.

We have told YOU a lot of things about Switzerland. Now we'd like to learn from you about your experiences here and your impressions of the Swiss and Switzerland.

The frame on the next page is for you to write about (or draw a picture of) your impressions of Switzerland or your Swiss friends or the places you have been that you like to remember. Or maybe we forgot to mention something in this book that you think is important for other kids to know who come to live here. We would be very happy if you could tell us that.

We will enjoy receiving your letters and pictures and we just might make a new book for kids like you that would include your letter or picture. So be sure to put your name and address on the other side of the page so that we can contact you if we decide we'd like to publish your work.

Don't forget that you won't feel at home anywhere in the world if you don't go out and get to know the kids around you. You only have to smile and say 'Hi'. Give it a try! We hope you discover lots of ways to keep ticking along with Swiss kids.

Send your letter or picture to:
Bergli Books
Ticking Along with Swiss Kids
Rümelinsplatz 19, CH-4001 Basel, Switzerland
e-mail: info@bergli.ch

Did you find all the bicycles? Look closely at pages 10, 18, 21, 25, 31, 40, 41, 55, 62, 70, 83, 110, 122 and 126. Tandems are counted as one so there are 21 in all.

My name is _____.

I am _____ years old.

I came here from _____.

I now live in _____.

127